TIPPERAR

By I

First published 2017 by TTG Publications

©Paddy McEvoy 2017

Revised edition, May, 2018

Cover photograph shows Tipperary Barracks

Acknowledgements

I thank the Christian Brothers without whom I might never have heard of the Punic Wars, or of the verbs that take the Dative case, among other valued inputs!

I thank all those people down the years whose penetrating inquisitions shook me to the foundations of my being, forcing me to question all that I thought I knew, and all they thought they knew. Those inquisitions put me in a solitary place, but I would be nowhere else. They it was who prompted me to embrace the maxim: 'Don't believe what you want to believe until you know what you need to know'.

Thanks to Dan Healy cfc for valuable feedback, to my niece Noeline for allowing me to use her stunning photo of our beloved Glen of Aherlow, to Christi for help with the cover and to Helen Coleman for her insightful observations.

Major thanks to John Young without whose unfailing support and intelligence this project may not have surfaced. Buiochas, fidus Achates.

And to all those dramatis personae that make their entrances and their exits in this factional work, without whose strivings on the world stage, there would have been no need for these speculations.

And to my wife, Fenney, for meticulous proof-reading and valuable advice, and to her and My Beloved Sons In Whom I Am Well Pleased for keeping me on my toes and being the fireproof cladding around my existence.

Paddy McEvoy, 27 09 2017

Also by Paddy McEvoy

Humanist Catechism for Young Thinkers:
Seven volumes in Amazon eBooks

A Disobedient Irish History:
Four volumes in Amazon eBooks

For more information and to buy:

https://www.amazon.co.uk/s/ref=dp_byline_sr_ebooks_1?ie=UTF8&text=Paddy+McEvoy&search-alias=digital-text&field-author=Paddy+McEvoy&sort=relevancerank

website: www.paddymcevoy.co.uk

This is a work of fiction. Names, characters, businesses, places, events and incidents are either products of the author's imagination or used in a fictitious manner. Any resemblance to actual persons, living or dead, or actual events is purely coincidental.

TIPPERARY IS AS FINE A TOWN

Chapter 1 ...History is a convoluted teacher...

Chapter 2 ...one Hail Mary short...

Chapter 3 ...War is declared...

Chapter 4 ...sed libera nos a malo...

Chapter 5 ...the letter...

Chapter 6 ...if London falls...

Chapter 7 ...Dan Breen to the rescue...

Chapter 8 ...the Taoiseach will see you now...

Chapter 9 ...a St Patrick's Day to remember...

Chapter 10 ...ranks close: veils are lifted...

Chapter 11 ...delivering butter...

Chapter 12 ...shorten the road...

Chapter 13 ...Antzies crawl...

Chapter 14 ...a Phoenix rises...

Chapter 15 ...benedictus qui venit...

Chapter 16 ...a strained stalemate...

Chapter 17 ...all you who are in love...

Chapter 18 ...Tipp'rary is as fine a town...

Chapter 19 ... old foes meet/the world turned upside down

Chapter 20 ...skeletons in cupboards...

Chapter 21 ...the naked Emperor...

Chapter 22 ...the truth shall set you free...

Chapter 23 ...the murder machine dismantled...

Chapter 24 ...a clash with the ash...

Chapter 25 ...Cuilin and Fachtna at the Aras...

Chapter 26 ...underground streams surface...

Chapter 27 ...the longing for a Homeland...

Chapter 28 ...O my Dark Rosaleen...

Epilogue: ...the Bonny Bunch of Roses. Their unity shall ne'er be broke...

Prologue

When what has happened has happened, we weave its narrative into a self-comforting web to catch the butterflies of probability. We interpret outcomes as part of some pre-arranged Plan, which we call The Narrative. We docilely go along with this as 'What Happened', but some schemers, often the least worthy among us, take carefully selected 'Facts', the 'facts' as they see them, to be a sign of Favour of some sort, be it divine, or fate, and twist all outcomes onto a self-servingly propitious new orthodoxy...

But we all seem, no matter what 'side' we find ourselves on, to crave the reassurance that God, or at least gods of some sort, are on our side, or at least, that 'we' are on the right side of history, or some such succour. We pour triumph and disaster down the same funnel of inevitability. We dismiss possible alternatives as inconvenient What Ifs. We see history as spilt milk, and the more sentimental of us cry a lot over it.

This extended essay is a What If, of sorts. In World War II, what if the Irish, or the Swedes or the Swiss.......But let's stick with the Irish for the here and now, and let the What-Iffers of those other countries deal with their own discomfiting confibulations.

The Irish have shed some sheaths in recent decades, but there are many more to go, in the quest for setting oul' Ireland free from the soiled, simplified, sadly blood-soaked 'verities' of the past. We are still in thrall to the 'hard man', the 'direct drive'- the grizzled 'ballot and bullet' operators who stop at nothing to get their way, barefaced fake-news manipulators who tell us simplistic hate-soaked whoppers, whoppers so big they leave decent people lost for words. They scream 'show us the evidence' whilst knowing all along that they, themselves, have 'disappeared' it down some forgotten bog-hole.

Well, those contrived circumstances were created in a particular context of distortions, in the historical hall of bendy mirrors. The fictional actors in this wee drama faced another, very real, hard man, who, had he prevailed, would have swept aside the half-baked myths of our own extremist political opinion-formers.

It's not only the external ideological propagandists we Irish need to stand up to. We need to stand up to our inner propagandist, challenge the mountebanks in our own conditioned minds who have played fast and loose with our gullibility. We need to tell ourselves some harsh home truths.

This is primarily for the young. It's also for the not-so-young, those who have never been comfortable with the threadbare tribalisms which have been imposed on us.

Why was this written? When I was at The Abbey Christian Brothers' School in Tipperary, I encountered the poetry of WB Yeats. These lines from The Fisherman helped me breathe...

………To write for my own race
And the reality:
The living men that I hate,
The dead man that I loved,
The craven man in his seat,
The insolent unreproved—
And no knave brought to book
Who has won a drunken cheer -
The witty man and his joke
Aimed at the commonest ear,

The clever man who cries
The catch cries of the clown,
The beating down of the wise
And great Art beaten down.

WB Yeats

The Fisherman

Chapter 1

...history is a convoluted teacher...

'Will this bloody lesson never end?' I muttered to myself. The teacher, McMehony, a man who exuded a flimsy self-importance, a misfit who should never have been allowed into that august profession, - ('twas said of him that he was a 'spoiled priest', a reject from holy orders), - would spend lesson after lesson, tediously dictating from his dog-eared notes, while we copyists strove to keep up with him. He was the sort of specimen, who when they announced that they had been teaching x number of years, might be reminded that they had been teaching one year, x number of times. Woe betide any poor eejit whose writing skills weren't up to scratch. Instead of typing the notes up and letting us have them in legible format, - he was too lazy for that, - he would instead drone on, day in day out, year in year out, and the devil take the hindmost. One of the boys one day said: 'Sir, what comes after France is the First of France?'

'I never said that'.

'You did, sir. You said something about someone inishee...inishee...something the rennaysans or something. He bought the Mona Leeza. You said that, sir'.

'Come out here and bring your scribble with you'.

The unfortunate scholar was dragged out in front of the class, and subjected to a barrage of abuse from the thug, and had to endure another chorus of ridicule from the sniggering smart set, always quick to jump on the bullying bandwagon, those who felt they were being held back, the Fainne-wearing, Pioneer-pin brandishing elite who were headed for pensionable jobs in the Civil Service, or teaching, or the Church - high perches where they'd be expected to know all about Francis 1 of France and the Renaissance.

'I never said France is the First of France, you empty-headed nincompoop'.

The poor boy was standing defenceless in front of the class, and forced to read out his unintelligible and illegible notes, to the hilarity of the A-streamers, and to his own crushing humiliation. He was one of the many who would fall by the academic wayside, and not appear the following September, if he lasted that long. Not in that school, anyway. If his parents had money, his torture would continue at Rockwell College, or Clongowes Wood, until the penny dropped, or the money ran out, and he wound-up back on the family farm, or in an English factory, or on a building site, depending on where he was in the inheritance pecking-order. 'You should join the Air Force, for you're no use on earth'; 'You should get a job on the railways – as a sleeper'; 'If you saw shells, you wouldn't guess eggs'; 'You wouldn't see a hole in a ladder'......' were some of the put-downs this poor boy and the rest of us had to endure in this hallowed hall of learning, etched indelibly in our collective memory.

Later on, the topic we were covering was the 30 Years' War. I was captivated by events such as the Defenestration of Prague, when the Emperor's emissaries were heaved out of a castle window, to land conveniently of a pile of manure, or so we were told. That great clash of visions over Europe's future that desecrated the lives of millions was to dictate not only our immediate school careers, but the course of the centuries to come, and not only in Europe.

'History is a convoluted teacher, boys. And it does not repeat itself, whatever some may say', McMehony would often say. 'Don't write that down. That's just my own opinion. And for god sake, don't quote me in the exam. Just quote the facts'. Ah....the Facts.

We were left in no doubt about which side 'we' were on, of course. We were always on the Catholic side, on Rome's side and agin' those pesky malcontent Protestants, be they English, Irish or whatever. Whenever Martin Luther's name came up, it was always uttered with contempt, and the fact that he married a nun, thrown in for good measure, to drive home the point that he was a thoroughly bad egg. There seemed to be some latent consensus abroad with Luther's more lurid declarations on the Jews, however. Neither did there seem to be any 'official' dismissal, at least no serious critique, of Shakespeare's portrayal of Shylock, the heartless Jew. I personally had reservations with this cosy consensus. To me, something major was amiss.

Living in a binary world, always having to be on one side or the other, Irish/English, Catholic/Protestant, 'normal'/homosexual.....was a burden to me. I knew there was a major flaw in these black-and- white, polarised ways of seeing things. This was the 1930s, just over two decades since the so-called Great War – that War to End All Wars- and in Ireland, two decades since the 1916 Rising and subsequent hostilities had taken place. And still, coming from both sides of the Treaty divide, the drip-feed of justifications was ever-present - one side elevating the revolutionaries Pearse and Connolly and their supporters, while the other side, staunchly defending Redmond's constitutionalism, while opposing armed insurrection, still had little or nothing good to say about the hated British. All the right arguments can't be on only one side, I thought to myself. That's not possible. My town had had a bad time from the Black and Tans in the early 1920s, the name having come from the colours of the local Scarteen 'Black and Tan' Hunt. Whenever there was a need to label someone, or some group, as epitomising total evil, the usual suspects were wheeled out, Cromwell, the Black and Tans, Henry VIII... But what puzzled me further was that in English lessons, often taken by the same teachers who hadn't a good word to say about the English when teaching subjects like History, we were presented with the sublime works of Milton, Keats, Shelley, Wordsworth and Shakespeare, and expected to exult at their 'harmonious cadences' and 'exuberance of phraseology'. (We were given these stock phrases, told to learn them by heart, and advised to drop them in 'casually' when we were answering exam questions on poetry appreciation in the Inter or Leaving exams. Any examiner who didn't smell a rat, when students from Inishowen in Donegal to Baltimore in Cork were parroting out the same deathless mantras, and who thought that students might be inventing these clunking infelicities spontaneously, would have left a lot to be desired as an examiner. But then, neither creativity nor originality were what the exams were about. James Joyce never got a mention, not as a writer, in any case, but as one of 'us', a Catholic, who had 'gone wrong'.

'The Bohemian phase of the 30 Years' War ended at the Battle of the White Mountain, which took place on Nov 8th 1620, outside Prague, when the huge army of the Holy Roman Emperor, Ferdinand II defeated the Protestant army of Bohemia, led by Christian of Anhalt......', McMehony droned on, as we scribbled furiously.

That war devastated Europe. It caused the deaths of hundreds of thousands, and caused hundreds of thousands more to abandon their god-forsaken home-places for the New World of America. What would Europe have done without the American bolthole?

'Where do I fit in, in all this', I would say to myself. It was clear to me that the tremors of that war were still being fought out on this very island, particularly in the northern part. A partial view of our own history had been pumped into us, about how the brutes from England had laid waste our land, right back to the marauding Normans, through the land grabs of the Plantation phase, the Penal Laws, the Boyne, the Famine.....the litany of crimes seemed endless, fuelling a moral indignation that seemed unarguable. Some of the boys would rage against the wrongs perpetrated on the poor defenceless Irish over 800 years, make that 1000 years, if you care to throw in the sadistic, rapacious monastery-pillaging Vikings. And with the pump of hatred being primed on a daily basis, it was no wonder the IRA had a steady stream of volunteers, and a steadier hinterland of 'sneaking regarders' – those who would make the right noises, sing the right songs, but were careful not to blot their copy-books. I often wondered if there might be something missing in my make-up that I didn't feel a Pavlovian response of instant irateness. Was there, perhaps, another dimension, a wider context, to all these stories that we were never being presented with? We Irish seemed to derive a certain solitary comfort from playing the oppressed victim. It also chimed nicely with religious sentiments.

There were people in our local community who had been deeply implicated in the War of Independence, or the Troubles, as the period was called. (These vicissitudes were always presented as having 'happened' to us, as if we played no generative part in making them happen.) Stories were whispered about certain men in the neighbourhood who had shouldered the gun, and most probably taken lives. Killing seemed to be so casually justified, particularly if it was a 'political' killing, provided the 'enemy' was a Black and Tan, a Tommy, an informer. The killing of 'one of us' was an outrage to be condemned, while a mealy-mouthed, disingenuous, fake-sympathy was forthcoming when the killing of 'one of them' was at issue. Alongside the hero worship of nationalist/republican demi-gods like Pearse, Clarke, MacDiarmada, etc., one heard others who were devoted to the cult of James Connolly and his dream of an Irish socialist utopia. There seemed to be no place for fence-sitting in our little town. You were either on one side or the other. If you seemed not to be 'sound on the national question', if you weren't consistently negative about the English, or the Northern Prods, you were quickly put in your place and reminded of how, and what, you should be thinking. The pressures to belong, to be part of the 'group mind', to be 'on board', to be 'one of us' were omnipresent. The Christian Brothers went to ridiculous lengths to Gaelicise everything, turning names that were clearly English into Irish names by adding an O' and, perhaps, lengthening a vowel. Some of the results were just embarrassing. There was general consensus that 'the Border' and/or 'the English' were the root of all our problems. If these didn't exist, we'd be all living in some sort of blissful El Dorado Tir na nOg. In no way was there anything amiss with ourselves or how we saw ourselves.

I made it my business to widen my cultural, political and historical horizons. I learned about First World War from an old neighbour who had served with the Connaught Rangers in that war. He had been shell-shocked, which affected his speech. He would button-hole me regularly, at night, like the Ancient Mariner to describe the horrors of the trenches. He would get misty-eyed and repeat names such as Passchendaele, Delville Wood. It crossed my mind that he hadn't been much older than I was then when he served King and country and fought for the 'freedom of small nations'. Except that the small nation he served was Ireland. But he knew a thing or two about war and from first-hand experience, something that McMehony did not, could not and never would know. We had a painting in our house of the Last Absolution of the Munster Fusiliers by Fr Francis Gleeson at Rue de Bois, before many of those men lost their lives at the Battle of Aubers Ridge in May 1915. Many of those adventurous young men were hardly out of short trousers.

And then, as well as the political, there was the religious dimension to grapple with. I see-sawed between phases of devotion and repulsion in spiritual matters. Again, you couldn't be so-so. You had to be fully-paid-up, or you were beyond the pale – hot or cold. The priests and Brothers liked repeating the Bible quotation from Revelations: 'So then because thou art lukewarm and neither cold nor hot I will spit thee out of my mouth'. These men were obviously red hot. They would say 'spit' with venom. I had a permanent feeling of being an outsider, alienated, looking in through my own wee window, on all this zealotry. When the Creed was said at mass, the congregation, as one, intoned the words: 'Credo in Unum Deum, patrem omnipotentem, factorum caeli et terrae, visibilium omnium et invisilibium......I believe in One god, Maker of Heaven and Earth.......'. And always in the back of my mind, I heard this niggling voice saying: 'Do I really believe all this?? Who has asked me if I believe it or not?' I had been expected to, told to believe. And I had been warned that if I didn't believe that I would go straight to Hell when I die. What sort of a deal is that?

Whenever our theological questioning got too technical for the Brothers, they would summon one of the local priests to come in to put us right. One such heavyweight we nicknamed Fr Gnash because of his passremarkable teeth. We would tackle him on hoary perennials like 'Who made god?' And: 'Did Mary really go up, physically, into heaven?' And: 'If she's up there physically, does she eat?' And: 'Have her clothes not worn out in nearly 2000 years?' Questions like those amused us, which Gnash, obviously, hadn't a clue how to answer. He always wound up by telling us that prayer was the answer to all those smart-arse questions, and we'd be better off concentrating on our lessons. He was very keen on short prayers, called ejaculations, and exhorted us to say them often, particularly in times of "temptation"'. His higher theology degrees hadn't prepared him for the more mundane interrogations he would get from iconoclasts like us. They certainly hadn't provided him with any answers. When he really wanted to bamboozle us he used words like teleological, eschatological, and apocalyptic. There's nothing quite like a fusillade of multi-syllabic words for silencing the uninitiated. We were reminded of the lines from Goldsmith's Deserted Village:

'....And still they gazed, and still the wonder grew
That one small head could carry all he knew....'

Gnash liked to tell us that God moved in mysterious ways when the going was getting sticky. One day he asked us if anyone had a question. I put my hand up. I could detect him bracing himself.

'Father? Can you explain what God was up to in sending the Angel Gabriel down to earth twice, once to Mary in Nazareth for the Annunciation, and 600-odd years later to Mohammad to dictate the Koran to him? Those two visits have well and truly put the cat in among the human pigeons, resulting in centuries of strife. Humanity may never recover from Gabriel's intrusions into human affairs'.

Whatever his small head contained, it was flummoxed by that question. I could feel bell, book and candle hurtling in my direction.

'I have one more question, Father'.

'What is it?' he eyed me suspiciously.

'Tell us about Sejanus?'

'Who?'

'Sejanus - the most powerful man in Rome during the public life of Jesus. He shared the consulship with Tiberias. Had Sejanus not fallen, the history of the time would have been very different'.

'Who told you all this? he demanded, his dander visibly rising.

'No one, Father: I can read. The time has passed when the likes of me depended on the likes of you for what we know'.

The silence in the room could be cut with a knife.

Too many of the Brothers were strap-happy, some to a worrying extent, leaving one to wonder what sort of kicks they were deriving from their promiscuous use of corporal punishment, but one of them in particular was a law unto himself. He radiated menace. Hearts skipped a beat when he walked into the room. His leather strap was bigger than the norm. He had a strip of lead sewn into it, to give it more heft. He seemed fearless of consequences. He would insult anyone in the school, or the town with whom he had the slightest quibble. He taught Maths. We were terrified of him. One day we were 'doing' quadratic equations. We had no idea what possible use they might ever be to us, except to get through the dreaded exam. One of the boys, taking his life in his hands asked: 'What are quadratic equations used for, Sir?' The ogre stared at him. Such a question could very well, and often did, result in a savage assault. After a pregnant and brooding silence he said: 'Do you know those aeroplanes they make nowadays, Boys?' 'Yes sir'. 'Well, they use quadratic equations to get them to fly'. Phew. Relief all round. Still not a clue.

And the same went for what I believed politically. Here we were in 1939. The Men of 1916 had declared for Germany in the WW1. They went as far as referring to the Germans as '....our gallant allies in Europe.....'. How gallant could they have been as allies when tens of thousands of Irishmen fought and died in British and Allied uniforms? Surely there must have been angles to this conundrum that never got an airing in the tunnel-visioned version of history that we were getting? We had been brain-washed at primary school with a heavy indoctrination of nationalistic songs and poetry that extolled the glories of dying for Ireland.

One song, however, struck a deep chord with me. It was a 1798 Ballad, the Croppy Boy. Its first verse went:

*'Twas early early all in the spring
The birds did whistle, aye, and sweet did sing
Changing their notes from tree to tree
And the song they sang was Old Ireland Free.*

Old Ireland Free? Old Ireland Free? Old Ireland Free from what - and free to do what? Our impossible dream.

It was dinned into us that the only way to set Old Ireland Free was to be prepared to die for it.

Dying for Ireland, or anywhere else, didn't hold any attractions for me. I just wanted to live. Not for Ireland, or for any other country. Just to live. And hopefully do some good while I was around.

Chapter 2

...a Hail Mary short...

'When will this confounded rosary ever end......?' Every night my parents insisted on saying the family rosary. Each of us had to say a decade, ten Hail Marys. I try to speed things up by cheating, chancing my arm with saying eight or nine. I can get away with nine, most nights, because no one is counting, because they don't want to break the rhythm, or because, secretly they want to get it over-with themselves. Nobody points out that I'm a Hail Mary short when I try it on with nine, but if I chance it with eight, depending on my parents' moods, all hell can break loose. On the odd occasion I've lost count and gone to eleven or even twelve, which was seen as deliberate provocation. My father, normally a placid man, can be explosive when aroused. The rosary itself takes about fifteen minutes, but the 'trimmings' as they are called can go on and on. Every dead relative who ever lived seems to be included, as does the Pope, the priests, the conversion of England, the conversion of Russia, as instructed by Our Lady of Fatima, the black babies of Africa, the cat, the dog......When I was staying with my mother's old relatives on a farm in Wexford, the woman of the house, who when saying the Lord's Prayer would say: '....and lead us not into tempatation....', asked me one night – 'Thomas, what does tempatation mean?' I thought she was joking. 'Are you having me on? You say it every night and now you tell me you don't know what it means?' She looked at me appearing to regret that she had asked, and said: 'Why would I need to know what it means? God knows what it means. That's what matters'. My parents weren't so trusting or blindly credulous as that but, if push came to shove, I'm not too sure....

Our kitchen chairs have spindle backs, parallel, like the windows of a prison, and my brothers and sisters, kneeling on the floor, would look across at each other as if from a prison cell, hands grasping the bars, wondering when our interminable nightly sentence would be over. When could we escape outside while there was a bit of light in the evening, to see our friends, play an hour of hurling, or in my case, when I got a bit older, some nights sneak away to see my sweetheart, Roisin. We had to be careful, through our respective cell windows, not to catch each others' eye, for if we did, a bout of giggling was bound to ensue. Giggling is contagious, and the myth of the family praying together, staying together is exploded and replaced with the family giggling together, niggling together. Some nights the rosary had to be abandoned altogether, the giggling having ended in meltdown, with uncontrollable teary-cheeked hysterics and incandescent parents glowering over their sacrilegious children.

I am prevailed upon, occasionally, to join in the rosary in Roisin's house, where I gain a different perspective into their take on that nightly ritual, the inclusion of aspirations of a much more political kind. Last year Neville Chamberlain came back from Munich clutching his fabled 'piece of paper'. Roisin's father added a trimming of his own, a prayer that Germany would come out on top in the inevitable war that was in the offing. He had been in the IRA during the 'Troubled Times' – 1916-23. When I asked why he backed Germany instead of England, he fixed me with a cold stare, wondered why I had asked, didn't I know what a nest of vipers the British were and why would I want anything else but the utter destruction of their stinking empire, their monarchy, their very civilisation – or what passed for one?

'Do you know what Gandhi said when asked about British civilisation?' he asked me. Actually I did know, but to humour him, I said I didn't.

'Tell me?'

'I think it would be a good idea', he guffawed as he spluttered out the answer. 'Pearse and Connolly were the boyos to put manners on those blackguards', he added, with malice. 'Now it's Hitler's turn'. I remembered what my old grandfather had said to me while he was alive. 'There are three sides to every story – mine, yours and the truth, and nobody's lying'. I felt that Roisin's dad was checking me out, as a suitable boyfriend. I had to pass certain tests, like in the old fairy tales. This shoehorning of my reality into ill-fitting, makeshift categories was an exercise I encountered too often, and which I felt distinctly uncomfortable about. I already had intellectual corns from the shoehorning that was going on with my schooling.

I had heard on the BBC news in 1938 an item about attacks on Jewish businesses in Germany. Kristallnacht it was called – the night of the broken glass. I mentioned it to Roisin's father the next time I was in their house and asked him what he made of it. 'Where did you hear about that?' he asked, pointedly.

'From the BBC'.

'The BBC' he retorted acidly, almost spitting out the letters. 'Surely you don't expect me to believe what you'll hear from that propaganda-sluice? Wise up, man' he said. 'Radio Eireann and the Irish Press are all we need around here to keep us right', he said. 'The truth in the news, an fhirinne sa nuacht. Don't be taken in by the farts that come from John Bull's arse'. Roisin was standing behind him and shook her head as if to say - don't push him. He could turn violent when his blood was up, and any mention of the English, the Northern Prods, the Cork hurling team, were always sure to raise his hackles. (Nor was he very happy about some of his old comrades who had done better than he had out of their service to the Republic, (or what passed for one), as I found out later).

'What are you being told at your home about listening to foreign lies?', he went on. Had I told him that the BBC was our main source of news, and that the Home Service was my mother's favourite radio station, he might have flipped, and made things very difficult for Roisin and me. So I didn't.

Roisin, on one of our walks in the Hills, had already confided to me that they were all in dread of him. 'My mother has to handle him with kid gloves', she said, 'and the rest of us tiptoe around him. When he gets together with some of his old IRA buddies, and drink is taken, some of the things I overhear disturb me' she said.

'Like what?' I asked.

'I know they killed people', she replied. 'I know by the way they look at each other that a lot is being left unsaid. They go so far in skirting around old campaigns, and then a silence descends. Most of them are on state pensions for their service. Some have done better than others, with jobs and even land, but they still see themselves as an elite of sorts. They blame the Economic War exclusively on Britain. Dev is a sort of god to them. The fact that the boat trains to Fishguard and Holyhead are constantly full with people whom this state has failed, doesn't seem to bother them, or even the fact that some of their own old friends have taken off to Britain or the USA. One of them keeps on saying: "Sure 'tis the best little country in Ireland". He thinks that's hilarious. I am very worried about people who are attracted into believing that violence is the solution to problems, political or personal, Thomas. To tell you the truth, I'll be glad to get away from home when I finish school.'

'I had another row with McMehony in school today', I told her.

'What about?'

'I got fed up with his lousy teaching and his lousier prejudices. When he has it in for a boy, he bullies him incessantly. We have him for English as well as History. We are reading Julius Caesar for the Leaving Cert. He insists on a particular boy always being the Soothsayer, while he, McMehony always has to be Caesar. You couldn't make it up. Anyway he pushes and jostles this boy Fintan Stoker, knocks him against the wall when he has to say 'Beware the Ides of March'. He is a time-serving leech who was rejected by the Church and gets paid to spout the party line, without an independent thought in his head. He was filling our heads with anti-Cromwellian stodge when I put my hand up. I asked him which side the Irish backed in the English Civil War. He looked at me suspiciously, for he knew he was hoist. If he said the Irish were on the side of the King, which they were, he would be contradicting the spew of anti-English, anti-royalty, anti-monarchy, anti-aristocratic bile he regularly comes out with. To have said we were on the side of Cromwell's republicans, which logically we should have been, would have been a lie. He slammed the book shut and stormed out of the classroom'. 'See me after school', he intoned, slitty-eyed. It wasn't a happy meeting.

'Why are you such an awkward bugger?' Roisin said. She would look at me in that way of hers that totally disarmed me. She was so beautiful I could cry. Whenever I looked at her I was put in mind of the lines from She Lived Beside The Anner ....

'Her lips were dewy rosebuds, her teeth were pearls rare, And a snowdrift 'neath a beechen bough, her neck and nut brown hair....'

I couldn't get my head around what it was about me that made that graceful girl want to be my girlfriend. I was still in my reverie when she said, quite aggressively: 'Are you listening to me, Thomas? Why are you always trying to unpick things?' This knocked the wind out of my sails, temporarily. I never liked it when Roisin seemed to attack me like this. What I daren't say was that when it came to unpicking, she wasn't bad at it herself. Except that I knew that in saying that, the conversation would have headed off in another direction entirely. I was learning when to bite my tongue.

'Well, as I see it', I replied, 'I'm not happy about what I'm being told to think. It seems to me that the Irish, because of their basic need to be approved-of, want it every way. We mistakenly see every enemy of Britain as being automatically our friend. Except that nobody takes us seriously because of our dodgy, self-serving historical analysis. We think that through the gift of the gab, and a dash of paddy-whackery, we can cover all bases. We are treated as a bit of a joke by the two nations that matter most to us, the English and the Americans, I fear. We were dragooned, down the centuries, by Rome and its placemen into siding with the Catholic, anti-British sides in Europe. This resulted in the Northern warlords inviting in the Spanish in 1601, the United Irishmen consorting with the French in 1798, and the men of 1916 kowtowing to the Kaisar , all doomed enterprises, because we knew in our heart-of-hearts that had any of those powers actually followed-through, occupied Ireland, and conquered England, that all-out war with Britain would have ensued, wars that would have devastated Ireland and left us much worse off that we were before they started. This reckless indifference of our warlords, temporal and spiritual, to the fortunes of ordinary people, has turned us into psychic punch-bags. Had the shoe been on the other foot, and the Irish happened to be the dominant power in these islands, and the English were the ones inviting in all and sundry over the centuries, how would we have reacted? With gentleness and sensitivity? I hardly think so'.

'I never thought of it like that before', said Roisin distractedly. I could see that she was getting fed up with my contrary thinking and wanted to get down to some serious courting. I could tell this by the way she linked arms with me, and sidled up close.

'What would have happened, for instance, had a sizeable, well-armed German army landed in 1916, which is what Pearse and Co wanted? What then? A blood bath the length and breadth of Ireland, that's what. The Shannon and the Liffey would have been our Sommes, the Bog of Allen our Passchdaele.'

'There's something radically wrong with you', said an exasperated Roisin, giving up on the courting and trying to forcibly withdraw her arm. But I held firm.

Chapter 3

...War is declared...

I had nearly two years of secondary school left when war broke out in 1939. People often ask where you were when you heard a wake-up, seismic piece of news. Hitler had invaded Poland on Friday, Sept 1st 1939. On the Sunday morning, Sept 3rd, I had been up early to go out in search of mushrooms for breakfast, a habit I had acquired since my days as an altar boy. I had been compulsively listening to the news on the BBC since the invasion had taken place. I was rooted to the spot when Chamberlain addressed the nation. An ultimatum had been issued to Germany to withdraw from Poland, an ultimatum which was, unsurprisingly ignored. Hitler had the Molotov/Ribbentrop Pact in his back pocket and wasn't worried about the bumptious Brits and/or the friable French. When my mother came into the kitchen, I was standing, as if electrocuted, petrified.

'What's wrong with you?' she enquired.

'England has declared war on Germany'.

'Sure what's that got to do with us? Eat your breakfast; you'll be late for last mass.'

What followed in our small town was extraordinary. As soon as the news had got round, we began to hear that prayers were streaming heavenwards, prayers for a sweet and swift victory, but a victory for whom? Why, for the Germans, of course. I couldn't believe it. Silt and sediment which had slowly settled was suddenly churned up by this lurch into the wilderness. An old neighbour of ours, a follower of Eoin O'Duffy, the Irish Fascist leader of the early 1930s, whose uniform was the blue shirt, and whose gangs were called Blueshirts, had her guttering passions stoked and would go on the rampage like an unguided missile, shouting 'Up Duffy', and bash you with her frying pan if you were unwise enough to come within swiping distance of her.

Roisin's father's blood was up too. He was cock-a-hoop to hear of the IRA's bombing campaign in England. The fact that seven unfortunates who were in the wrong place at the wrong time were slain and nearly one hundred injured, didn't seem to bother him a whit. 'Merely collaterals', he said, whatever that meant. The fact that they were English seemed to be enough to justify the outrage, even to mitigate its wrongness. 'What must it be like, to live with a murderous heart?' I thought to myself. Sean Russell, an IRA leader, who had been part of the bombing team, hot-footed it to Germany to declare his loyalty, and that of the IRA, and probably and delusionally the Irish people, to the Fuhrer. The Irish Taoiseach, de Valera, caught between jagged rocks and flinty hard places, decided on a policy of strict neutrality. Ireland was to tread an artful path. The country was a moiling hotpot of pro- and anti- British factions; pro- and anti- German factions; still pro- and anti- Treaty factions; unionist, separatist, pro- and anti- neutrality factions... there were belligerents and pacifists, socialists, fascists, reconstructionists and anarchists, all in contention, and all dividing and overlapping in unpredictable and messy ways.... Dev opted for what seemed to be the safest course, the 'plague-on-all-your-houses' option', that of neutrality. Had he known what was going on in Axis territories, and not just in relation to Jews, would he have done the same? What did he know? Whatever he knew, he conveniently chose the tactic of employing the deaf ear and the blind eye, the classic box-clever position.

But as time went on, stories began to trickle through of thousands of Irish people deciding to join the Allies. There were even stories of serving Irish military personnel, despite grave forebodings, abandoning their posts and donning the uniform of the old enemy, to the consternation of some. They were being described as 'deserters'. Only in language-mangling Ireland, I thought, would volunteers opting to run towards a war, rather than away from one, be described as a deserter! The country was divided in every way possible.

McMehony was having a field day. 'Will it be a German or a British invasion, boys?' he would declaim, smirking, safe in the knowledge that we were sitting pretty, come what may. We knew full well what answer he favoured. The thought of either scenario coming to pass, particularly the first, filled me with a chilling apprehension. McMehony seemed worryingly energised at the thought of German boots goose-stepping up Bridge Street.

The Government sprang into action on Sept 2nd 1939, proclaiming The Emergency. Emergency legislation, called the Emergency Powers Act 1939, enacted the following day, gave the government a sweeping range of powers, including the internment of those who had committed crimes, or of those who might commit them; the opening and censoring of mail; the censorship of the media. It was an authoritarian's dream come true.

I was taking a keen interest in goings-on in Europe, much to the mystification of schoolmates, who seemed to be in a state of moral paralysis, not knowing what to think, but being careful that whatever they thought, the boat should not be rocked. . There was widespread admiration for what Hitler had achieved in the 1930s, about how he had instilled a sense of national purpose back into the German people after the humiliations of Versailles. There was the occasional voice saying: 'If only we had a Hitler here, we wouldn't be in a state of economic stagnation. We wouldn't be worrying about the Economic War or about pot-holes and gumboils, that Hitler would sort out the farmers and construct a decent road network throughout the country'.

Germany invaded Norway in April 1940 and France fell in the June of that year. 'What'll happen if he invades England?' I asked my friends. 'He'll be welcomed with open arms', some said. 'Sure wasn't Edward VIII a great fan of his? Isn't he still? He'll be reinstated as king, for starters, and the present royals, who are German, after all, them being only latterly dubbed Windsor, will get the same treatment as the Romanovs did in Russia if they as much as squeak. They can always get jobs down the mines helping with the war effort'. One heard quite a lot of such dismissive, brutal, hare-brained wishful thinking.

I couldn't understand how complacent my friends and fellow townsfolk could be in the face of such a potentially imminent and impending catastrophe.

Churchill came to power in April 1940. This development pleased me a lot as I had been taking an interest in this man's actions and speeches for some years. I read somewhere that there was a question mark over his mother Jenny's background, that she might have been part Jewish? Was this partly the reason why he was hell bent on destroying this pestilence that was Hitler, before it was too late? He could clearly see that Hitler, who had no respect for truth, was up to no good. Churchill had been advocating the building up of the armed forces to rearm against Germany, while appeasement was more fashionable among the elitist in-crowd. But who can be blamed for trying to avoid war? To fail to be prepared for its inevitability, in the face of a double-dealer like Hitler, is another matter.

'If only', I thought, 'if only Churchill were to offer a deal to de Valera – an end to neutrality in exchange for an end to the Border?'

I thought that this would be a visionary offer. It would kill so many tough old birds with the one stone: finally, there would be the uniting of Ireland; the taking of Ireland of its place among the free nations of the earth, that aspiration which had cascaded down the centuries from the mouth of Robert Emmet; the expansion of the Irish economy; the end of the Economic War, that folly of Dev's that had crippled the country; the incorporation of unionists' energies and goodwill into the orbit of Ireland's affairs; the ending, once and for all, of any need for para-militarism, terrorism, armed struggle, sectarianism, and a plethora of other nasties that have bedevilled the island/nation of Ireland for centuries.

But would de Valera bite, if such bait were dangled before him? Could he be persuaded that Ulster's Unionists could, or would be enjoined to come on board with the plan?

I felt myself slipping into a mental slough of dissociation, of estrangement. The Ireland begotten by the New Order of 1916 was increasingly becoming an intellectually stifling place, a backwater of moral brutalism. There seemed to be no-one in my circle who saw things as I did, or if they did, they weren't letting-on. I felt I was so much at loggerheads with status quo thinking, at odds with the cosy orthodoxies of church/state overlaps. Did I even want to stay in this place? I had no one to talk to.

Except, that is, for my beloved, my Dark Rosaleen..

Chapter 4

... sed libera nos a malo...

I still attended the odd mass, and many of them were very odd indeed, - just to keep 'the mother' happy. My father didn't seem to notice or care. I could never quite fathom what he thought about religion, or of what passed for religion in our country. I knew he had very little time for the priests, even less for the bishops, whom he accused of feathering their own nests first, and tightening their grip. He had major problems with such powerful men owing allegiance to Rome, first, and not to Ireland. It was said that de Valera sent a draft of the new 1937 Constitution to Rome for approval. The Pope's verdict? 'We do not approve. We do not disapprove?' One could detect the thumbprint of such absolutist casuistry right across the whole tapestry of Irish life.

My father whose name is Hugh, would talk of what he called the recent 'phases' of Irish history particularly the modern periods since about 1700. The first phase, in his analysis, was that of what he called the Landlordism of the Soil, when Ireland was saddled with the post-Cromwellian aftermath, when the landlords from their eminences in the 'Big House', and backed by a phalanx of repressive Penal Laws, and armed force to back them up, lorded it over the common, mostly Catholic peasantry. Then came the post-Famine phase, from about 1850, when the Catholic Church stepped into the breach as spiritual NCOs of the nation, slowly replacing the old patronising aristocracy, and settled comfortably into the driving seat. This phase he called the Landlordism of the

Soul – the phase we are still living through. But this second phase wasn't all altruistic public service and catering to the people's spiritual needs, these Landlords of the Soul had managed to commandeer great swathes of Ireland into Rome's property portfolio, in a relatively short slice of time. Their knuckles will have to be whacked off that property, just like was necessary with the last lot of usurpers. The struggle to wrench their horny hands from control of the schools, in particular, will degenerate into embarrassment in the end. But he thought that this phase too will end and the next phase will be the Landlordism of the Spirit when the people will finally take their own destiny into their own hands, free from intrusive and patronising agencies, of this or of allegedly higher worlds, bullying them into following imposed scripts. While some other nations have been able to evolve relatively freely, the Irish have been trussed-up mentally, saddled with a history which has left them intellectually stunted and morally retarded. (When I say this in certain circles it goes down like a lead balloon.) Who do they have to thank for this spiritual equivalent of Chinese foot-binding? The landlords of soil and soul, that's who. The people have been bonsai-fied, the motto being 'snip the roots, clip the shoots'. (I had come across a copy of the Vatican Index of Banned Books. Censorship was alive and well in the Ireland in which I was growing up. The Church, having infantalised the people, proceeded to berate them for not being mature enough to be trusted with an 'unapproved' book, which the Church in its wisdom had deemed unsuitable for unsophisticated minds. And so the merry-go-round whizzed pointlessly round.)

All of these buffetings and batterings were impinging on me as I turned up for mass on that Sunday in late 1940, as London was being blitzed. I was lost in my thoughts, letting the archaic Latin waft over and through me, for although I was by then not a believer, I loved that spare language and its power to get directly to the point: 'sed libera nos a malo - deliver us from evil'. There was a lot of evil to be delivered from during those worrisome days.

The priest, the bould Gnash himself, mounted the pulpit to deliver his sermon. 'In this month of November we remember the suffering souls in Purgatory', he began. (These suffering souls were the lucky ones, of course. The unbaptised weren't so lucky. They were cast into eternal oblivion, forever deprived not only of the sight of God in the next life, but of a Christian burial in this one, like the unfortunates who had taken their own lives.) The congregation, who had varying levels of awareness of the rampages of the Nazis through Europe, many of whom had families and relatives in England, shuffled uneasily. For them, at that turning-point, the goings-on in Purgatory wouldn't have been high on their agendas. 'By saying six Our Fathers, six Hail Marys and six Glory Be To the Fathers, we living Catholics, members of the Church Militant, can exercise the great privilege of having the soul of a loved one who is languishing in the cleansing fires of Purgatory, a member of the Church Suffering, released to enjoy the glorious vistas of Heaven, to join the ranks of the Church Triumphant. The important thing is to go outside the church after every phase of six prayers – eighteen in all – the soul won't be released unless you actually leave the church and go out and come in again. That's how it works.' ('How does he know?' I wondered to myself. In my younger years, when I'd first heard this, I felt an exultant sense of power that I could exercise control over the comings and goings of souls trapped in Purgatory. It gave me a heady feeling to know that there were souls in Heaven who were there because I had sprung them from Purgatory. The sight of these prayerful shuffling conga crocodiles were a wonder to behold. A visiting anthropologist who happened on this bizarre scene would have marvelled at the sight and wondered what the hell could be going on.)

I was lost in my inner conversation as Gnash droned on about the poor suffering souls. I wondered how much more of this gobbledegook I could take when a man stood up – right in the middle of the church, which was something unheard-of and said quite audibly - not shouting – 'What about the poor suffering souls in England, you blinkered idiot. Never mind your Purgatory which probably doesn't even exist?' He shuffled out of his pew, pushed his way through the latecomers at the back and left the church. There was a stunned sense of disbelief as the priest's jaw dropped. Things like that didn't happen in our town. He passed quite close to me, allowing me to get a good look at him. I recognised him as a worker in the local creamery, named Tim Enright. For a split second I was on the horns of a dilemma. I knew I should react, but what to do? I followed him out of the church. I walked beside him in silence for a while.

'That was a brave thing to do', I said.

'Brave or not, I'm sick to death of those moral mountebanks, with their deals and their pacts – with France, with Spain, with Mussolini, with Hitler. Last week one of them was telling us there would be no trouble if all the warring factions, both Allies and Axis powers, were to kneel down and prostrate themselves before the Blessed Sacrament to worship it; Jews, Muslims, Hindus, Protestants, Catholics, atheists – the lot. Sometimes I wonder what planet those well-fed parasites inhabit, with their best houses and fancy cars. They are beneath contempt. They make no distinction between the Nazis and their enemies, the Allied Powers. But I know what they're about, the conniving chancers. They're hedging their bets in case Hitler wins. It's an old strategy of theirs. How do you think they have managed to survive for two millennia? They see Communism as a greater danger than Nazism. Maybe they're right. But for the ordinary person, particularly if you're Jewish, it's like having to decide between leprosy and cholera.'

I introduced myself. 'I know your family', he said. 'I went to school with your father'. I was elated by what he was saying. Here was a man, many years older than myself who had summed things up more or less as I saw them.

'Are there others in town who share your views?' I asked.

'Not many', he said, 'but I have a few friends who see dark clouds on the horizon. The Irish think that Hitler will go easy on them if London falls, but I wouldn't bet on that. The Germans regard us as untermench, like they do a lot of others. They're not fooled by our fig-leaf of neutrality. If they come here, and I think they will, we're in for the rudest of awakenings'.

We arranged to meet on the following Wednesday evening, in the Hills. We were joined by a few of his friends, some of whom had served in the British army in the First World War, some of whom were ex-IRA, but all of whom viewed an Allied defeat and a German-dominated Ireland with deepest foreboding. Although I was shocked by the gloomy prognosis of these people, I was strangely comforted to know I was no longer alone in my summation of things.

I listened as crystal-clear thoughts were exchanged calmly. These people knew their history, and their political antennae were impressive. 'So, what do we do?' I asked tentatively. Being by far the youngest, I was expecting to be patronised, but that was not the case. 'Are you at school still?' one of them asked. I told him I was. 'And do you have that gobshite McMehony teaching you, the golfer?'

I said I did. He rolled his eyes. 'God help you'.

We agreed to meet regularly to swap notes on matters arising. We were all listening to the BBC World Service,

Radio Eireann and the Irish papers being full of the usual mushroom mulch – keep them in the dark and tell 'em nothing.

I wondered if I should tell them of the letter to Mr de Valera which I was putting together. I decided to take the plunge.

'I've started a letter to de Valera' I began, 'setting forth my opinions on the neutrality question, among other matters. I'd be interested in your thoughts on what I have to say'.

'I wouldn't be expecting very much from him', said Austin, an ex-IRA man. 'His only job, as he sees it, is to negotiate the ship of state through the rapids of Irish politics for the duration of this mayhem, to keep the people in the dark by keeping the lid on the convulsions that Europe is going through, and hope that things will get back on a even keel when all the madness is over, whoever comes out on top. He knows full well what's going on, between briefings from the Vatican, and from that specimen of an ambassador of his in Berlin, Bewley, as nasty a piece of stuff as ever wore shoe-leather. He's a Jew-hater. Much more could have been done to save Jewish lives by allowing them into Ireland were it not for him. He's one of those people trying to be more Irish than the most officiously Irish, a dangerous and slippery breed'.

'Bring it along on Wednesday', said Tim, humouring me a bit I thought, a 'sure-it-can't-do-any-harm' tone in his voice.

News of Tim's remonstration in the church had spread like wildfire through our close-knit community.

People were taking sides.

Chapter 5

...the letter...

Dear Taoiseach,

You don't know me so there's little point in long introductions. My name is Thomas Sheehan. I am from Tipperary. My ancestor, Patrick Sheehan from the Glen of Aherlow, was the subject of Charles Kickham's ballad about the Crimean War.

Mr de Valera, I implore you to read this letter.

I believe that Ireland, and Europe, stand at a T-junction. One path leads to perdition, the other to liberation. I believe that Ireland has made a fatal error in opting for neutrality in the present war, which we are euphemistically calling an Emergency, making us a laughing-stock among those facing extermination. This is much more than an Emergency, Sir, this is do-or-die. By opting for non-combatant status, we are making ourselves look naïve at best, opportunist at worst, among the peoples of the free world. I am well aware of the unhappy relationship we have had with our near neighbour for centuries. How could I not be, after ten years of Christian Brothers' history? But now is not the time to dwell on past grievances but to rise to this unprecedented challenge. I believe that many rewards will come as a result of our taking sides in this holocaust: self-respect, international recognition that will endure and stand out from history books yet to be written and also, Irish unification will be a prize. We cannot be denied the latter goal, and whatever objections that have been put forward by our unionist neighbours, they will be deemed null and void if Ireland shoulders its burden in this conflict.

Ireland, with a 10,000 year history of settlement, was anciently a distinct entity with a language, a literature, a legal system and a culture that ran the length and breadth of the island. (On the matter of the language, may I say that the so-called 'revival' policy of the government is an utter, total disaster, wasteful of scarce public monies, and likely to drive more nails into its already battered coffin. I say this as a secondary school pupil. Teachers are a disgrace for electing to be complicit in it. If they chose to opt out, as a matter of principle, this misguided policy would founder.)

Were it not, particularly for the Plantation of Ulster, I believe Ireland would have held together as a unit, however imperfect, but a unit nevertheless. I also believe that were it not for external European factors, artfully exploited by the Catholic Church, Ireland would have more warmly embraced the Reformation and the intellectual hinterland that came with it. Sadly, the people who arrived in some numbers, the Planters, in the 17th century, and their descendants, unlike the earlier Normans, clung together as an entity, and never bought into our native ways, which is an ongoing challenge for the 'majority' population, and a task for the future, to be achieved by civility and neighbourliness, not violence.

By your actions in 1916, and those of your comrades, you succeeded in sundering this island. It would, in my opinion, have been far wiser to have delayed the plan to break with Britain, until there was consensus on the nature and shape of an all-island, all- Ireland settlement. Now, Mr Taoiseach, is your opportunity to put right this terrible mistake.

You personally escaped the firing-squad, because of your alleged American birth. The British, not wishing to antagonise the Americans, spared you. (It was also said of you that you were spared because of your being of lesser importance.) If London falls, and the Germans come here, as they surely will, they cannot be relied-upon to have the scruples of the British and spare you, particularly if you do as I beg of you in this letter, the Allies having collapsed. I read that it was even considered in 1916 to invite a German prince to be King of Ireland. Can this be true? Hitler won't be installing a king, as he will do in Britain, but he will surely have a puppet.

Ireland has been disfigured by violence, by para-militarism, by browbeating and gangsterism, North and South. I'm sorry to say so, but the type of person attracted to violence I find disconcerting, however noble the aspirations. People who opt for violence, like you did, when slow-moving constitutional methods exist, set young people like me a very bad example. Will you be encouraging your own children to take up the gun, Mr de Valera, or do you see the job of nation-building as a task completed?

If we give up neutrality, it will have to be on the publicly-stated and internationally-binding understanding that we are doing so, first and foremost because of our opposition to fascism. And second because of our insistence that Ireland be rid of the Border, that excrescence that scars the face and soul of our country. I believe the British will go along with that. The fulminations of the Unionists (in my view bogus - who would they have gone to war against - the very people they wished to stay in 'union' with?) - should never have been acceded to. But the Ireland that will be a home to one million Protestants will have to be a very different place to the Free State which currently exists, re-thought from root to branch. Hitler will go through this island like a dose of salts. If the Czech and Polish borders meant nothing to him, he's not going to be deterred by a customs-post in Strabane. No, if the Germans invade us, they will not be interested in the nuances of our Border. Hitler doesn't recognise such niceties. Anyway, what good will it do any of us to have Ireland united under the Swastika? This is a grotesque proposition, but so deluded are some of our zealous fellow-citizens, that I believe the thought has some allure. To be united is their fantasy, under any flag, in any circumstances. These people are extremely dangerous. Their wishful-thinking has led them down some strange paths.

Such an undertaking by the British will cause consternation among Unionists in Northern Ireland. There will be those among them who will shout "Lundy' and accuse London of selling them out. Tough! They should have been taken on aggressively since O'Connell's time, certainly since Parnell's. But they weren't. Why? Because of delusions of grandeur by people like Churchill who thought that not only did the sun never set on the British Empire, but that the sun would never set on the British Empire. While the empire loyalists were only too ready to trumpet the fact that Britannia rules the waves, those of us on the receiving end were quick to point out how readily Britannia waives the rules, when it suits her. The Ulster unionists, under a Dublin man Carson, should never have got away with their antics at the time of the Treaty. Some will threaten to leave, some will actually leave Northern Ireland, as many did, regrettably, in the south after the War of Independence, (many unwillingly, to our shame). We cannot help that, though I don't wish to see anyone go. But if the reason for their leaving is their intolerance of the Irish, or our culture, or the Catholic religion or our traditions, what on earth are they doing in Ireland in the first place, deluding themselves that they are where they are not? Their opportunistic forebears came to Ireland with a hostile, supremacist agenda, which still lurks in the psychic undergrowth of many of their bigoted minds. Good riddance to such narrow-minded people I say, if they choose to go. I only hope they don't hawk their bigotries elsewhere as they did throughout the world. (Toronto, for instance, has a massive Orange Day on July 12th.) The vast majority of the decent Ulster Protestant people will throw in their lot with a unified Ireland and the South will be all the better for having them on board.

The Irish Constitution, that confining document, will need to be amended to grant the freedoms that Protestants demand as of right. This will put the Catholic hierarchy's nose out of joint. Also tough. They and their ilk have ridden roughshod over the tender sensibilities of the biddable Irish for far too long and this is a golden opportunity to dethrone them, these 'princes' of the Vatican. It is time to create a level playing field for all citizens, for all faiths, and none, in the Ireland of the future. How quick, how willing the aristocracy of the Church were to assume the airs and graces of the old aristocracy! 'My Lord; Your Grace; Your Excellency.' The use of aristocratic labels such as these in a country calling itself an embryonic republic should never have been tolerated. These titles had been jettisoned at Independence, or so we thought! Between the spiritual powers-that-are and the British, the Irish people have been left in a morally weakened, intellectually stunted, socially infantilized and politically immobilised condition. There are great challenges ahead for us in the 20th century. Are we equal to them?

Are you equal to them, Mr de Valera?

With this post-War settlement, there will be no on-going role for the IRA or for any of its gangster offshoots – no smuggling across the Border, because No Border. No role for Loyalist paramilitaries, because their raison d'etre will have disappeared, their fox well and truly shot. What a gain for Ireland and for future generations! No longer can 'respectable' politicians, or populations, hide behind the menaces of their armed foot-soldiers, appearing to condemn them, on the one hand, while secretly giving the nod to their gruesome deeds, on the other. These ambivalences have weakened us morally as a people. You can't half-believe in violence. Ask Hitler.

The New Ireland, taking its place among the enlightened nations of the earth will wipe away forever, the slur of the treacherous Irish, who were not to be trusted as a neighbour. (There is much knee-jerk denial of such accusations in the Irish psyche – more evidence of moral and political underdevelopment? Perhaps you will baulk at this characterisation yourself?) Historically we dallied with the Spanish, the French, then the Germans during WW1 – all prepared to use us as a back-door to attack and to destabilise Britain. Whatever the reasons and the contexts of those times, these mutterings, these finger-pointings, both at and about us will in the future be null and void as Ireland declares its true persona by siding with the civilised, liberal nations of the earth, (mainly Protestant as it happens).

You must know, Mr Taoiseach, what is going on with the Jews in mainland Europe. The Irish, who know better than most what it is like to be the abandoned of the earth, must act generously towards these wretched people. The suggestion that only those Jews who converted to Catholicism be allowed in to this country is an abomination, and unworthy of a nation calling itself Christian. You, who are greatly respected by the Jewish community, must face down these anti-Semites.

There are those who say we are defenceless, that we will take a pounding if we declare for the Allies. And they are right. But we shall be defended by the Allies while the war progresses, and even if London falls, we shall still be on the right side. Yes, we will take a pounding – like Dublin did in 1916, and for what? But that pounding will wake us up out of that self-pitying slumber we currently wallow in. If the Germans take over here, and we come to know what life under the Swastika is like, we may very well look back ruefully at life under the British and question the hysterical exaggerations of people like Pearse and his hyperbolic Murder Machine rhetoric. On the subject of murder machines, the Nazis are the Murder Machine par excellence, Mr de Valera. We've seen nothing yet. When all the chaos and carnage is over, as over it will be one day, Ireland, if it chooses wisely, can take its place among the decent nations as a modern, open country, fully-qualified to belong to the free world.

I urge you to expel all Germans who have come here as 'lovers of things Irish, the language, the music, the culture'. Many of them are Nazi party members, or at least sympathisers. I have heard of one such in Donegal, in Carrick and other fishing villages, who goes out in the fishing boats, taking soundings of the depth of the harbours with his plumb line. I wonder what he needs that information for? He has done this in other harbours down the western seaboard. We Irish are putty in the hands of anyone purporting to love our neglected language and song. As long as the bottle of whiskey is produced, we'll sing till morning. There are some of them in high places in the museums and folklore centres.

I am a school student, Mr de Valera. I am writing this as the Luftwaffe pulverises the south of England. I get my information from the BBC, as Radio Eireann is as informative as a head of cabbage.

Ireland's opting for neutrality is seen internationally as a hedging of bets, which, let's face it, is precisely what it is. We did make a commitment, at least the authors of the Proclamation did, to our shame, in World War 1, for Germany, while our own gallant sons - over 200,000 of them, nearly 40,000 died - were stepping up to the plate to give the Hun the run. I believe that thousands are currently crossing the Border and others heading for England to fight the Nazis. When this war is over, if we don't choose correctly now, they shall be our saving grace, to clutch at some straw of honour. I hope that the members of the Irish Armed forces who have changed into Allied uniforms will be treated with the respect they deserve, when the time comes.

Disastrously, in 1918, the big mistake made, by the Allies was not in pressing home their military advantage, but instead they allowed a stalemate, called an Armistice, which deluded the Germans into thinking that they had not been defeated, when in reality, they had. Victory over Germany should have been declared, an honourable peace negotiated, not the unexploded bomb that was Versailles, and Germany allowed to rebuild with dignity. Had a generous and fair deal for Germany been agreed, Hitler and his cronies may never have seized power, which may result in the deaths of millions before this chaos is over.

There are already hundreds of thousands dead or wounded, Mr de Valera. Do the honourable thing, join the right side, demonstrate that Ireland can maturely recognise real evil and erase the confused memory of 1916. Ireland and the world will thank you.

Neutrality, for a country in our situation, with our long, sometimes troubled association with Britain is a casuistical fig leaf. Please let's have done with weasel words. The English people, and the Allied nations, will never forget our bigness of heart in coming to their aid in their hour of need. Now is not the time for sitting on the fence, or for walking by on the other side.

Slan go foill

Thomas Sheehan

Chapter 6

...if London falls...

I took the letter along with me on my next date with Roisin. I told her I had been meeting up with Tim Enright and some others. Her face masked what I knew were internal worries. Roisin asked if my parents knew.

'No', I replied. 'They are really non-political people whose only wish is for an easy life. And who can blame them? There are already too many people in this country who are infected with either one of the twin viruses of zealotry or inertia. Millions in Britain and Europe want a peaceful life, too, but they're not going to get one'.

'Thomas', she said, a note of real alarm in her voice, 'I'm becoming seriously worried about all this. You're still at school. You don't even have the Leaving Cert behind you, and here you are, writing to Mr de Valera - de Valera no less - about Irish neutrality, for God's sake. It's not right. I'm not sure I can take all this. Why not leave it to those who are in a position to do something about it? What sort of life could we have, with you getting involved in such matters?'

I could see the tears welling up in Roisin's eyes and I felt my heart swell for love of her. We had been together for nearly two years now, and to me she was everything. She had colonised my soul and I felt incomplete when she wasn't around. When I caught sight of her, unexpectedly, on the street, my heart raced, and it was as if a light had come on inside me. Sometimes the love I felt for her unsettled me. I had had no idea that one person could feel so permeated by another. 'Can this get any more intense?', I would wonder to myself. The person I had become since meeting Roisin was a different 'me' to the old 'me'. I began to understand what being 'born again' meant. I heard people use the expression 'hopelessly in love'. My love for Roisin, on the contrary, filled me with hope.

'What do you mean?' I asked her. 'Are you saying you don't agree with me?'

'You know I agree with you, insofar as I understand you', she said. 'Have I ever rejected outright what you think? These are such big ideas; I need time to take them in. Things are not easy at home. My father has been talking about Tim Enright's outburst at mass. If he knew you were in cahoots with him, life could become very difficult for me. I'm not in a position to break with my family, Thomas. Not yet. Not ever, I hope. I'm sick with worry.'

'But the letter Roisin, what did you think of the letter?'

'I think it's a great letter', she said. 'If it had been me writing it, I'd have said that references to God should be removed from the Constitution. There should also be something about the predicament of women in Ireland. The old slogan, 'Keep 'em thick and keep 'em pregnant' should have no place in a modern country'.

'I'd prefer to stick to the neutrality issue', I said. 'All those issues are for another day'.

'If we ever get through what you think is going to happen, you'll be hearing from me about these and a lot of other women's matters. Did you know that girls disappear in this country? The pregnant ones are put into those dreadful laundries and are treated like slaves or they escape to England. Even if they are just a bit wild in their behaviour, they can be put in institutions. These are bad places. These are bad times'.

'I agree. We will follow those matters up in the future, Roisin', I said. 'I promise you. I can't wait for those days.'

Our eyes met. 'And I can't wait for the time when we are together, forever'.

'What do you mean, Thomas?' she probed.

'You know very well what I mean', I said. I held her close and the power of our love passed between us like a jolt of electric current. My thoughts at that moment were anything but neutral. Roisin was putty in my hands and I in hers. The intensity of our feelings for each other melded us into one. On my walk home, the travails of the poor suffering souls in the war seemed worlds away.

When I next met with what was now becoming a growing and increasingly important circle of friends on the following Wednesday, we discussed the letter. I had asked my aunt, who worked in an office in town, to type it up for me and to make copies.

'Much will depend on how the present air battle in England goes', Tim said. 'So long as England holds out, Dev will do nothing, which, of course, highlights the moral, not to mention the military incongruity of Ireland's position. If London falls, and the Germans invade, there's going to be one hell of a scrap throughout this island, particularly in the North which is already on a war footing. I cannot imagine the Americans not getting involved as they see the Nazis tighten their vindictive grip on all our throats in the event of Britain's collapse. And knowing they are next'.

'I am going to get the letter to the Taoiseach, in any event', I said. 'Whatever the outcome of present hostilities, the question of the bona fides of Ireland's present neutrality policy remains. History will have something to say about our response at this imperilled time, questions along the lines of the: 'Ireland, what did you do to stop Hitler?' variety.

Most present agreed. One member, Dan Buckley, said he had problems with the bit about the Irish supporting the Germans in WW1. 'The Irish were never asked', he said, 'no more than they were consulted about the Rising itself. Between cabals of bishops and secret societies, we are treated like a flock of sheep in this backwater. Who can blame the people if they behave accordingly?'

I did remind him that I included the many thousands of Irishmen and women who had stepped up to fight for the freedom of small nations.

'Any other scraps of news?' asked Tim, who by now was looked upon as the de facto leader of our ad hoc committee of sorts. There were now about 20 of us.

One of the men said that the priest who had enraged Tim was making trouble, spreading rumours. 'Don't take any notice of that eejit', said Austin. 'He's the buffoon who got in a tangle about the rotten apples'.

'What rotten apples?'

'One Sunday he was hectoring us about how sinful we were and about how the people of the town needed to show each other good example, particularly the 'big shots'. He started off by saying, "If you put a rotten apple into a barrel of good apples, the rotten apple will turn all the good apples rotten". He repeated this a few times, for effect, to let the message sink in, before he hit them with his tour de force. Then he rose to his full puffed-up chest-expanded magnitude and brandishing his finger, declared: "But take heed of this, dear brethren. As Holy Mother Church teaches us, if you put a good apple into a barrel of rotten apples.....' He then hesitated. He went over these lines a few times, mostly to himself, realising he had tangled himself up...He eventually lowered his finger, before the congregation descended into paroxysms of laughter. "Devotions this evening will be at half-past seven", he said and scurried from the pulpit, tail between legs, beetroot red'.

That raised a chuckle or two.

'Is that everything?'

'Only what I heard from that renegade scum Lord Haw Haw', said 'Gildi' Arkwright, an ex-British soldier who had settled in the town and married a local girl, after the departure of his comrades in 1922. 'I tune in to him occasionally to remind me of what we are up against. He has many supporters in these parts, to our shame.'

'I get the impression from reading between the lines that Allied casualties in the Battle for Britain, which it should properly be called, (which is also the Battle for Ireland, by the way), are getting higher and higher. The new Dark Age that Churchill spoke about in his House of Commons speech could well turn out to be a reality if air defences are overwhelmed. If the RAF can withstand daily losses of aircraft and aircrew, then, as Churchill said, it will surely be their finest hour, but we mustn't fall prey to wishful thinking, - that all will be well - however beguiling it is. I had a letter from my brother in the States who told me that Joseph Kennedy, the US Ambassador in Berlin was reported in the American press as being very pessimistic about Britain's hopes for success. In fact, Roosevelt is reported as being keen to have another opinion. Kennedy, another dubious latchyko with a defeatist attitude is no friend of Britain. Or of Ireland, for that matter, for however deluded many Irish seem to be, if England falls, Ireland falls. Kennedy is clearly more interested in being the first Catholic president of the United States, than in hoping for a British victory. Could he be playing a long-term, self-serving game with regard to Hitler, hoping to assume the presidency and then to go easy on the Nazis in a subdued Europe, leaving us all in the lurch? I hope I'm not offending anyone here but I do get the impression that

Catholics in the main are much less exercised in opposing the Nazis that I believe they should be.'

No one in the group said a word but there were many nods of assent. They had seen through the veils of obfuscation woven by Church biases.

'Do you mind if I ask you a question, Gildi?' I asked.

'Go ahead'.

'Where did you get the name Gildi?'

'Glad you asked, Thomas. I served in India. I was always complimented for how well turned out I was. The Indian soldiers, who pronounced it as if it were spelled with a J, Jildi, gave me the nickname Gildi. It's a Hindustani word, I believe, for someone who is always immaculate in appearance. And look at the state of me now. But I'm as happy as a pig in muck.

On my way home, I called on Roisin. She knew my knock.

'What do you want?' she said. 'It's after ten o'clock.'

'I want you to do me a very big favour'

'What is it? she asked, eyeing me suspiciously.

'I want you to come to Dublin with me'.

'And what would I want to go to Dublin with you for?'

'I want to deliver the letter to de Valera in person'

'Are you completely mad?' She sounded at the end of her tether.

'Roooooooiseeeeeeeeeeeen', I heard her father bellow, none too invitingly.

Chapter 7

…Dan Breen to the rescue…

When we arrived at Kingsbridge Station in Dublin on Thurs 2nd January 1941, the city was in uproar. Earlier that day, the German Luftwaffe had dropped bombs in Terenure. To the utter dismay and consternation of the Irish, bombs had also been dropped in counties Meath, Wicklow, Carlow and Wexford.

Everybody in the city was talking thirteen-to-the-dozen about the bombings. Excuses and explanations were ten-a-penny. We listened to the exchanges on the buses. 'Pilot error', went one line of explanation.

'How could the feckin' pilots be that far off course?' came the rejoinder.

'They're scaring us in case we re-think our neutrality policy in the event of England's collapse '. 'That's a funny way of keeping us in our box. If they know anything about the Irish, they surely know that bullying us is no way of putting manners on us.'

'I think it's intentional'.

'Why would it be intentional? They know full well that we'd be far more likely to pray for them than for John Bull'.

We enquired about how to get to the Dail, and were directed around Trinity College and up Kildare Street, to Leinster House.

There were two Gardai on duty outside the Dail, Burly and Lanky, we named them afterwards. We were asked by one of them what we wanted. When we told him, he looked as us with open-mouthed stupefaction. 'To see who?' Burly intoned with disbelief, his voice hitting falsetto on the 'who?' 'These two from Tipp are here to see the Long Fella', he said to his fellow custodian. (He pronounced 'what' as if there was a 'p' and an 'f' in it – it sounded like 'pfwhat' that rhymed with 'cat').

'We have a letter for him'

'A letther abou' pfwhat?' (He sounded as if he was from the Wesht).

'It's private', said Roisin, a note of resigned despair in her voice, as if to say, We've come all this way to be belittled by these patronising, self-important, uniformed nonentities. We stood there deflated.

'Sure Dev isn't even here today', Lanky said. 'Do you know what's goin' on here at all, at all? We got bombed by the Jerries last night, so we did. He'll be over in Terenure, pressing the flesh, puttin' himself abou'.

Just then a man passed by and one of the guards said, 'There's yeer man'. 'Who?'

'Dan Breen, one of your Tipp TDs'.

'Mr Breen', he shouted, 'can you help these young constituents of yours?'

'What do they want?' He enquired gruffly, I thought, in a flat, unmusical voice. 'We have a letter here for Mr de Valera'.

We were now face-to-face with the fabled Dan Breen, hero to some, gunman to others. He had taken part in the notorious incident at Soloheadbeg in 1919 when two constables were slain, an outrage that had precipitated the blood-letting of the following four years. It was well known that Breen's sympathies were with the pro-Axis powers in the present conflict raging in Europe. I'd heard some weird rumours about his current associations, but now wasn't the time to put a foot wrong.

'A letther about what?' There was an intimidating tone to his voice. He sounded as if he was interrogating us. 'You should know that if you want to have any business with the government that you have to go through me, your elected representative. What're your names?'

My name meant nothing to him, but when he heard Roisin's, he took notice.

'We've heard all about you, Mr Breen', I said, hoping to plámás him.

'Have you indeed?' he said, lightening up a little, assuming that what I'd heard, I approved of. 'I'll tell you what I'll do. Mr de Valera will be here early in the morning. I know that. If you come here at 7.30, I'll see if I can get you in to see him for a few minutes. Give me the letther and I'll see it gets delivered to him this evening. I gave him a sealed copy of the letter, but I kept the original in my inside pocket. Just in case.

'Go raibh maigh agat, a dhuine uasal', I said in my best Christian Brothers' Irish. 'We'll be here at 7 o'clock in the morning'.

Roisin had an aunt living in Rathmines who would put us up for the night, so we took off to see the sights of Dublin with whatever was left of the day. First on our list was the National Museum. I wanted to see the exquisite gold work that predated the arrival of the Celts to Ireland by nearly two thousand years. I pointed out one particular piece of beaten gold to Roisin. 'When do you think that was made?' I asked her – 'don't read the label yet'. 'It's obviously Christian' she said, noting the cross at its centre.

'Now read the label'.

'Early Bronze Age Gold', she read out, '2400-1800. That's about 2000 years before Christianity came to Ireland', she said, perplexed. 'And it's got a cross at its centre. How can that be?'

'It's nearly 2000 years before Jesus lived. Don't be relying on what the nuns are telling you, my love', I said, 'no more than I rely on the Brothers for my knowledge, with their blinkered and biased version of Irish history. The cross is common to the iconography of most cultures, as are a host of other symbols. The Christians commandeered it as they did many other beliefs and practices. It's an old trick of new brooms in history – assimilating and absorbing ancient, native traditions. Did you know, for instance, that the swastika – that hated symbol of the Nazis, is an ancient Sanskrit symbol? It symbolised good fortune until Hitler got his hands on it, and turned it clockwise 45 degrees?'

'I never knew that', she said.

'Stick with me' I said elbowing her, winking. My heart quickened and I felt more alive whenever I looked at that girl's flawless face.

We climbed to the top of Nelson's Pillar. We had a brilliant view of the GPO, where the 1916 Rising had taken place. I imagined the state of O'Connell Street after the mayhem had finally stopped, after the 'terrible beauty' was born, afterbirth splashed all over the place. Roisin said she couldn't believe she was actually at the very spot she had heard about so often. She was amazed that the Pillar had survived all the bombings and shootings. O'Connell, at one end of the street and Parnell at the other, had ironically been trenchant advocates of non-violence, the direct antithesis of the insurgents' methods. The GPO stood equidistant from each of them, but the actions of the men in the GPO were a violent repudiation of the life work of those two great Irish parliamentarians as the bullets whizzed round the heads of the statues. Looking down on this iconic street, I thought to myself: 'What if the German arms and personnel had arrived? The destruction would not have ended with the city centre.

We made our way up to Rathmines, looking at the Book of Kells in Trinity College on the way. Roisin was so appreciative of all she was encountering, which pleased me so much.

On the bus out of the city, I thought of the destruction of London and feared for the fabric of Dublin, Belfast, Waterford, Cork, Limerick, Tipperary, if our shield in London buckled.

When we had exchanged pleasantries with her aunt and family, we prepared for our important meeting the following morning. I carefully re-read the letter to Dev before going to sleep, to be ready for a barrage of whatever was to confront us on the morrow.

Chapter 8

...the Taoiseach will see you now...

We were up at six o'clock the following morning. We listened to the news on the BBC. Roisin's aunt and uncle were puzzled by our intense interest in such far-distant matters.

'Sure what do you want to be bothering your young heads with all that dreadful business for?' the aunt asked us. 'And what in the name of all that's holy do you want with Mr de Valera? Don't you think he has enough on his plate?'

'We'll let you know if anything comes of it', I said. 'It's just a project I have in mind, which I think he might be interested in'.

'If it brings a few jobs to this benighted country of ours, I'm sure he will', her uncle said.

'Can I hear just one more thing on the radio at 6.30, before we go? I asked.

'Go ahead'

I tuned in to Reichssender, Hamburg to hear the unmistakable drawl of Lord Haw Haw, William Joyce, with his fake upper-class English accent, intoning the words: 'Gairmany calling, Gairmany calling......'.

'I often listen to him', said the uncle. 'Sure he's one of our own, a Galway man'. Joyce, born in America, had been educated in Ireland. He dabbled in Fascism and made himself scarce in August 1939 when he feared being interned by de Valera.

Haw Haw was particularly menacing on this particular morning. 'The RAF is on its knees. The British are finished. Britannia has run aground. The British bulldog is toothless. The invincible and overwhelming might of the Luftwaffe is destroying airfields, installations, and ordnance, shipping, ports, any enemy position that hasn't already been destroyed, on land and sea. It is only a matter of time before the brandy-swilling, cigar-munching Churchill, for all his empty bravado waves the white flag, and gets on his knees to Herr Hitler.....Gairmany calling Gairmany calling......'.

'Sure I wouldn't be inclined to take too much notice of that old windbag', Roisin's uncle said. 'It's all propaganda. Just like the BBC. They're all at it'.

'But just for arguments sake', I said, 'just suppose for a moment that he is right. After all, the Nazis are rampaging through Europe. Towns and cities have been overrun and whole countries have been jackbooted. Why not London?'

I could see he was increasingly uncomfortable with this possibility. 'Sure if they come? So what? The Germans have no axe to grind with us nor had we with them. It's Churchill's scalp they're after, that same bucko - no friend of Ireland's, not now, not in the past – he's the one they are after. And wasn't Lloyd George a great buddy of Hitler's, though he seems to have changed his tune of late. I wonder why? And what about Edward VIII, not to mention the press magnates of Fleet Street, more big buddies of Hitler, so he can't be all bad?'

I could feel we were on boggy ground. There was a strong sense of being dug in coming through what he was saying, and to prolong the exchange was to risk seeming ungrateful for their hospitality. We proffered our gratitude, wished them slainte mhaith and made our way to the bus-stop. We alighted at St Stephen's Green and walked over to the Dail. The same two guardians of the national threshold were there again.

'Well, look who's here', they joked, 'and at sparrow fart'.

They were under instructions to allow us in. Then a porter took over and accompanied us up the impressive central stairway to the Taoiseach's office. We were told to take a seat on the bench outside.

'I don't think I should come in with you, Thomas', Roisin began.

'Why shouldn't you?'

'What use will I be to you? What do I know about all this stuff? There are times when I feel I am in so far out of my depth, I don't know what I'm doing or saying. My parents think we're on a short trip to Dublin, to see the sights, before school starts back on Monday. And here we are, trying to change Ireland's policy on neutrality, for God sake! It's mad, Thomas! There are times when I feel I should break it off with you, that I'd be better never to have been drawn in to all this'. I could see she was panicking.

'Jesus, Roisin', I said, 'your timing is unbelievable. Here we are, about to meet the most important man in Ireland, and you choose this precise moment to break up with me. I can't believe it'. She was shaking, and by now, so was I.

My eyes pleaded with Roisin not to abandon me. Not now.

The door opened and a man came out.

'The Taoiseach will see you now'.

We were ushered in to an imposing office, to be confronted by the most famous face in the country. Mr de Valera looked austere but kind, with those distinctive glasses and long face. He shook our hands and invited us to sit down.

'You are welcome to Dail Eireann', he said in a subdued but courteous voice. 'You may thank Mr Breen for arranging this meeting. I am not in the habit of shoehorning-in unscheduled visits'.

He asked us about ourselves and took great interest in our studies.

'I have read your letter, Thomas. I have read it with great interest. And then I re-read it. Tell me, did you write it yourself?'

'Yes, Sir', I replied, my heart doing cartwheels in my chest.

'What age are you?'

'Seventeen'.

'When I was seventeen, I was playing rugby, carving my name in college desks, and enjoying myself. And why, may I ask, are you so interested in these grave matters?'

As I groped to put language on the tumult in my mind, Roisin piped up, the words gushing from her mouth, not her usual delivery. 'He never stops talking about history and politics, Sir. He reads all sorts of books and materials. I tell him he'll never pass his Leaving Cert, because the sort of things he knows are not on the syllabus. He disagrees with what you and your fellow insurrectionists did in Easter Week 1916. He says you'd have been better off to have heeded O'Connell, Parnell and Redmond. He doesn't have much time for Carson, but he says that we could have got a deal after the War that would have kept Ireland from being partitioned. He says that in staging the Rising when we did, that we threw away our greatest bargaining chip, the thousands of brave Irishmen who gave their lives for the freedom of small nations. The Unionists never seem to stop going on about the sacrifices made by their side. Why shouldn't we?'

I thought my head would explode.

'Does he indeed?' said Dev, warming to the conversation. 'And does he say anything else about me and my comrades?' I felt as if I were a fly on the wall – about to be swatted.

'He says you are a mystery man, that a shroud of secrecy hangs over you, that it is said you may even have been born in Ireland, or at least taken away as a baby'.

'Jesus, shut up Roisin', I thought to myself, hoping the floor would open up and swallow me. I couldn't nudge her or he would have seen me.

'All will be revealed in the fullness of time. What was it Balthasar Gracian said? *"Truth always lags behind, limping along on the arm of time."* A wise man! Now Thomas, tell me about this letter'.

'Well, Sir', I stumbled, 'first, can I say Thank You for seeing us. As far as I can tell, London is on the brink of defeat. You must know this. I believe it is a question of when, not if. Before this happens, we, that is, the Irish government should be ready and poised with our response. As far as I know, this government has no credible contingency plan in such an eventuality. Granted we have a Local Defence Force play-acting throughout the country, vicariously acting out what real soldiers are doing all over Europe. What deterrence or resistance could they provide if, or more realistically, when the Germans invade, as they have done in Poland, and throughout Western Europe? I believe that the Molotov/Ribbentrop Pact will collapse, and that Hitler will invade Russia when he has mopped-up these islands. I believe that these events are imminent and inevitable. When he has consolidated his hold on Europe and the Middle East, with Italy marauding through North Africa, and Japan menacing the Pacific, I believe that America will have to decide what to do.

I plead with you to pull the plug on the neutrality policy. Now! Immediately! The reason for the urgency is that if we delay, it will look like opportunism of the worst sort, that we are only doing so because our backs are to the wall. This is no time for opportunism, an expedient that Ireland is too well-noted for. Our backs were always to the wall, but because we banked on the Allies holding the line, we could take what we deemed to be the moral high ground, safe in the knowledge that we were being protected. It is a pusillanimous, ambivalent position to adopt, Sir. There will be resistance to Germany throughout the British Isles, as there will be here. I can't believe that there aren't many more raised voices putting forward these arguments, other than Mr Dillon and a few others. Are any in your own Party putting pressure on you to act with urgency? When the Germans land, if Ireland hasn't previously nailed its colours to the mast of civilisation, we shall be a laughing-stock when the Nazis are finally defeated, as defeated they will be, as they must be. There is no way that the Third Reich will last a thousand years. I don't give it a thousand days. It is rotten and riven from top to bottom. What was it that Jesus said? By their fruits ye shall know them. Well, the fruits of this madman are bitter and poisonous in the extreme.

I heard on the radio this morning that London seems to be hanging on by a thread. You could and should, and must, bring the Irish people with you by a mature appeal to the better angels of our ancient and noble nature. For, what is the alternative? To say that the Germans are decent and honourable? That they would be welcome here? That they are still 'gallant allies' of Ireland?

The Germans cannot hold Europe from Valencia Island, through Russia to Vladivostok. There will be an awful reckoning and Ireland has a narrow opportunity to climb aboard the right bandwagon. If we choose wrongly now, it will haunt us forever. I know we have justifiable grievances against England, but now is the time to show the true nobility of the Irish folk-soul. I believe that there are huge dissensions in the German High Command, whatever Lord Haw Haw says'.

'Oh, you know about him?' He said, looking surprised. 'My, you are keeping up with things', he said, more icily now, I thought. 'But, you surely don't believe all that stuff you are coming out with. Who is informing you? I'm afraid our time is up. I've given you much longer than I intended. Before we finish, though, I'd like to ask the young lady what she thinks about all of this.'

'Thank you for asking, Mr de Valera', Roisin said. I wondered what she was going to say. 'We have been told in our History lessons of the brave, mostly men, who died for Ireland. Our generation has been fed a stirabout of patriotism and piety. We have been taught songs like God Save Ireland.....

'Whether on the scaffold high or the battlefield we die,

O what matter, when for Erin dear we fall?'

Do you think this kind of message is appropriate for young impressionable minds, Sir?'

'And yet you are here, asking Irish people to die for something else?'

'If you can't distinguish between re-defining our relationship with Britain, and standing up to Hitler, we really are in dire straits'.

He looked seriously taken aback.

'We all die of something, Sir, having first lived for something. I'm going to be a doctor. My heroes are Elizabeth Garrett Anderson and Eleneora Fleury, the first two women to qualify as doctors in these parts, and above all, Millicent Fawcett. Millicent Fawcett didn't go along with the violent antics of the Pankhursts. She took a different path, a slow burn. And it was her guiding light that won the vote. Constance Markiewitz is constantly held up to us young Irish women as a role model. That is wrong. Fawcett is a much more inspiring role model. She it was who suggested to Sir Hubert Parry to put Blake's poem Jerusalem to music. She was inspired by the words: 'I will not cease from mental fight, Nor shall my sword sleep in my hand, Until we have built Jerusalem, In England's green and pleasant land'. For England, substitute Ireland, substitute anywhere. Blake was no parochialist. There has been too much emphasis on 'freedom from' at the expense of 'freedom to' in Ireland. 'If we were free from England, all our problems would be sorted', goes the mantra. Wolfe Tone's 'Break-the-connection with England' catchphrase is hard-wired into the brains of Irish people. Well, Mr Taoiseach, in my opinion, that is a great lie. Would Napoleon have been preferable to King George? There are many fine aspects to England and to the English people that never get mentioned in the torrent of hot-air invective that keeps the Irish nationalist balloon in the air. And what is the outcome? It keeps us from maturing as a people. Narrow-mindedness holds people back. I shall give my life to medicine and to women's rights, as well as to those I love and care for. It is far too easy to give a death. To give a life requires real sacrifice. My personal motto is: Be Brave. Behave.

We are death-obsessed in Ireland. I blame the Church for this. By fixating on death, they maintain their macabre control over the people.' (I began to fear that she was going too far at this point.) 'One guiding principle in maintaining order-of-a-sort in this country has been to let sleeping dogs lie. But the problem is that hungry dogs wake up and don't require a kick to turn vicious. How many unsolved crimes are there in this country – serious crimes? Has anyone been prosecuted for the burning down of the old Barracks in Tipperary, for instance? Do you care about that or about all the other crimes? States founded on violence are inherently unstable. If the governance of a country doesn't command the consensus of the vast majority of the people, weaknesses in the body politic persist'. (This speech left me dumbfounded.)

The Taoiseach intervened. 'You're somewhat of a female Machiavelli, aren't you? You are obviously heavily involved in these matters', he said.

'Not involved, committed', she answered back, as quick as a flash. 'My father says, it's best explained by the relationship between eggs and bacon. With eggs and bacon, the chicken is involved - but the pig is committed'.

'But the pig gives his life'?

'No, the pig's life is taken. The challenge that confronts us now is a much more far-reaching one than that of insurrections and assassinations and snipers. The very fate of civilisation hangs in the balance this time. When your neighbour's house is burning down, it's time to man the pumps, not be engaging in idle speculations. It is vital we make the right decision.'

Dev stared at her in silence. 'Thank you, Roisin'. He said. 'So, where do we go from here?'

It was my turn to speak. 'The question is: Where do you go, Mr Taoiseach? The options are extremely limited', I said. 'We'll be going back to Tipperary. But to let the world know how the thinking of the vast majority of the Irish people is moving, I have already sent copies of my letter to London, Washington and Belfast'.

I could see he was getting tetchy. 'Are you a member of some organisation?' he asked. 'No, Sir', I replied, 'just a loose grouping of friends who see eye-to-eye on the grave matters which are arising, to use your own word'.

Dev stood up.

The meeting was over.

Chapter 9

...a St Patrick's Day to remember...

The news in the early months of 1941 could not easily be censored nor contained. Letters were arriving daily from the Irish in Britain with personal, doom-laden accounts that many aspects of national life were under severe strain, some even at breaking-point, that links were weakening: in the media, in social, administrative, military, and in educational services. Hospitals could not cope with the surge in casualties. People began to arrive back to Ireland in significant numbers. Those who had left in the '20s and '30s, disgusted by the failure of the Irish 'revolution' and the ravages of the Economic War, of the inability of the so-called 'forces of liberation' to provide employment, housing, medical services, security, - people who had benefited from Britain's relative economic stability, Depression notwithstanding, now that the country was on a war footing, - were deciding that it was safer to live on the bread-line in Ireland than on the front-line in England, where they risked imminent annihilation either from bomb or storm-trooper.

It was not difficult to read between the lines in the media. It could not be said overtly that the end was nigh, but it didn't take a forensic genius to work out that the end of the beginning was indeed nigh, that the dam was about to burst.

There was an announcement on Radio Eireann that the Taoiseach was to address the nation on March 17th St Patrick's Day, at 3 o'clock. This would give all those who had been involved in the Parades time to get home to hear what Mr de Valera had to say. There had been much public comment in the early months of the New Year about how the Allied war effort was going, not forgetting the fortunes of the Axis forces. The Russians were suspicious that if Western Europe fell, Hitler would turn his fire-power on them. There was no love lost between these bastions of totalitarianism, be they fascist or communist. The only conundrum was to work out which one feared or hated the other more.

The downward spiral in the state of Britain's security was appearing more often in the pages of the Irish papers, as was the realisation dawning of what Ireland's response should be if, horror of horrors, London should fall. The Irish Times and the Irish Independent were carrying a growing range of articles questioning the morality of neutrality in the circumstances that were prevailing. That stratum of Irish society, not blighted with a knee-jerk anti-Britishness, those who had generally supported the Treaty, (a majority, incidentally), knew where their priorities and obligations lay.

The usual suspects, those on the Left and republicans, could be relied on as always to trot out the predictable and maddening mantra about England's difficulty being Ireland's opportunity. This banal raking over cold ashes was increasingly being countered by pragmatic voices who could see further than the confines of the threadbare arguments of the past, and ask what sort of opportunity does the fall of London really provide Ireland with? An opportunity to welcome in the Nazis? Surely this would herald the scraping of the barrel of our moral dissolution?

Speculation was running high about what Dev would say at 3 o'clock. Would it be about the war? If yes, what? Would it be about the bombings or the Local Defence Force or refugees? Is he going to call a snap election? Is he going to resign? Is he going to increase child allowances.......? Every working wireless in the country was tuned into Athlone.

What he had to say was a bolt from the blue.

'A dhaoine uaisle', he began, 'I send my warmest greetings to you all on this St Patrick's Day, a day when Irish men, Irish women and Irish children the world over remind ourselves what it is to be born into this unique Gaelic family of ours. This is the day we proudly wear the shamrock, that symbol of our deeply rooted Christian civilization. Wherever in the world we may be, from Galway to Dublin, via New York, San Francisco, Sydney or Bangalore, or from Derry to Kerry via the North Pole, the Pacific, Antarctica or Africa... we exult in the appellation Irish man or Irish woman. And long may it continue to be so.

But it is not to issue the usual Le Le Phadraig felicitations that I am speaking to you today. You will all be keenly aware of the perilous times we are living through, that the tap-root of European civilization is being poisoned by the evil philosophies of fascism and communism. But our immediate threat is fascism. To pass by on the other side, and pretend that our neighbour does not need our help, here and now, would be to fail the Man from Nazareth. At the onset of the present European Emergency, the Irish government declared its intention to be a non-combatant nation. This was interpreted by some as being ambivalent in our analysis of the rights and wrongs of the current European and world situation. Ireland has suffered too much throughout its history to be naïve about the rights and wrongs of war, and the dire implications of war. But Ireland knows that had the Munich Agreement, signed between Herr Hitler and the then British Prime Minister

Neville Chamberlain, been honoured, the present Emergency would not now confront us. Ireland also knows that it was not the British who dishonoured that Agreement, but Germany, just as it was Hitler who invaded the Rhineland in 1936 in violation of the Versailles Treaty. These are truths which we Irish should have the candour to face up to. I am in receipt of daily bulletins from our London Embassy of the finely-balanced, even deteriorating, state-of-affairs our neighbour Britain finds itself in. Washington is also in daily touch, and Washington will not stand idly by in the event of the military demise of Britain.

For this reason, I hereby announce that as of today, Ireland abandons its Neutrality policy and declares its unequivocal support for the Allied cause. The Treaty Ports will be made immediately available, if needed. American warships are ready and waiting to respond to orders to sail, when the time is right. Ireland shall no longer dither, waiting to decide what to do, while the skies over the south of England are darkened by aerial combat in which the Luftwaffe seems to be gaining the upper hand. We are declaring what our principles and priorities are, here and now, today.

Ireland, from this hour, until the scourge of Fascism is extirpated from the face of the globe, is on a war footing. Neutrality is ended. There will be some of stunted moral outlook and of a politically warped mentality who will rail against this abrupt change of policy. Suffice it to say, it has the unequivocal support of all members of my Cabinet. We had only three resignations. If any dissenters from the government's new policy cause trouble, they will be contained, as have some other malcontents who egregiously and irresponsibly seek to undermine the peace and good order of our fragile state, with its many challenges. The people who are most vociferous about Ireland being too unstable to act with good authority are the very people who will be first to challenge and subvert that authority. The judgement of these people is impaired by their obsession that the perfect is the enemy of the good, an aphorism we have all something to learn from. We may well have Nazi feet on Irish soil in the coming months. And shame on any Irish man or woman who joins with them or gives them succour. It would be improper to go public on the undertakings that I and my Cabinet have received, but take it from me that when this nightmare is over, Ireland's Border will be no more. It is an irony that the very country, Germany that played its, admittedly very minor, part in the dismemberment of this country, will now play a significant role in its re-membering. There is international assent to the plan that when Hitlerism is no more, Ireland, that spier-bhean of the Aisling poets will be as one, that our Four Green Fields will be embraced as one entity. Therefore there will be no more need for private armies, republican, loyalist, or any other breed of dissenting cabals on this island. Beidh Eire, aris, aige Cait Ni Dhuibhir. If there are any in the Six Counties, I shall not call it Ulster because it is not Ulster, who cannot accept this eventual settlement, a settlement which a wiser and fairer London should have ordained decades ago, they will perhaps reflect on their continued residency on this island. This will not be our choice, but theirs. A long and noble tradition of Irish Protestants who supported Irish nationhood gives the lie to that despicable falsehood that to be Protestant is to be automatically anti-nationalist, anti-unification, and pro-unionist.

This policy-change represents a watershed in the dented fortunes of Ireland. When these coming days are but a poignant memory, like all the rest of our many such, we can hold our heads high among the proud and free peoples of the earth. We can and shall, join commemorative events as equal partners, both here and abroad. We shall finally and properly, honour those Irish men who volunteered in World War 1 and who, to our collective shame, have been dishonoured. We are and should be as proud of them and their heroic sacrifice as the people of the North are of their doomed youth. We shall, as well as seeing German troops among us, also, in time, see Allied troops. This we shall have to accustom ourselves to, in the solid knowledge that the latter will be temporarily billeted here, which I can't promise about the former. There will be damage, there will be suffering, but there will be generous economic aid to give an injection to the economy, which, as we are all so painfully aware, it urgently needs.

This decision has been arrived at, not from any external pressure, but from the internal pressure of our informed consciences. Radio Eireann will play solemn music for 48 hours to give us all time for prayer and reflection. This is no time for hysterical voices or grandstanding gestures. This is a time for calmness. And if you do decide to pray, pray for something which a loving and caring God would wish for this suffering world. You might, for a few moments in your meditations, imagine you happened to be born Jewish, and on the mainland of central Europe. Our choices are stark and there are no fudges in the offing.

I am grateful to those who have helped me and my Cabinet to come to a position of clarity in our thinking on these labyrinthine matters, but to some young people in particular, who confronted, in my own case, my blinkered thinking - about whom, more anon. As one of my mentors Balthasar Gracian said many years ago: 'Truth limps along behind, on the arm of time'.

Dia's Muire's Padraig dhibh go leir. La Fheile Phadraig shona dhibh go leir.

A stunned silence descended on the farmlands and boglands, on the highroads and bohereens, on the hedges and ditches, on the pubs, on the town squares, on the homes, on the streets of Ireland, streets which only hours before had been enjoying Carnival, Irish-style. The simple import of those words percolated through to the very folk-soul of the people. Here were words that the people knew, in their heart-of-hearts, to be overdue, liberating words that needed to be uttered. And now they had been spoken.

People saw each other as if for the first time, as if the skin of an old phase of their collective being had been sloughed-off, as if a film had been removed from the soul's eye. The old self-pitying, melancholic victim-persona, so long nurtured by the Irish, lay in tatters at their feet. If the Irish knew what it was to be dehumanised, they also knew how capable they were of playing that game.

It was invigorating. It was intoxicating. It was heart-stirring. It was a re-birth.

It was all our aislings come to fruition.

Chapter 10

...ranks close...veils are lifted...

The British army had been beaten back to Dunkirk in June 1940 and men had died in their thousands. A rickety armada of every craft available had rescued a sodden, shelled, shocked and shattered remnant of an army and ferried it back to English terra firma. Over that winter the Luftwaffe pummelled the southern counties of England as the Heer, the German ground forces, smashed through all defences. They landed at multiple points of the coast of Britain on July 1941 and overwhelmed what remained of the depleted defence forces of the country. The Surrender was announced after fierce fighting on July 15th St Swithun's Day. The old superstition about rain on St Swithun's Day lasting 40 days was recalled. People prayed that the Nazi reign would last no longer, but they knew they were praying to a god that had sent the Nazi's in the first place. Miracles were not expected. Town after town was overrun. Quisling elements crawled out of the woodwork, some of whom had been expected, some not. The Daily Mail, owned by Lord Rothermere, a staunch ally of both Mussolini and Hitler, was in a feeding-frenzy of ecstatic self-congratulation. Rothermere had written an article in 1934 entitled Hurrah for the Blackshirts. He also owned the Daily Mirror which showed its true colours. The Daily Express, true to form, likewise welcomed the Nazis.

Belgium and the Netherlands had fallen in May 1940 and the euphoria of invincibility coursed through the veins of the pumped-up Germans. What they had expected to be stout defences fell like skittles.

England had not experienced such internal chaos since 1066, when William the Conqueror had stormed through the country like a hurricane, scything through all opposition. The experience of being overrun by a foreign invader was one which was alien to English experience. As wounds were licked in hamlet and thorp the length and breadth of the country, minds were cast back ruefully on all the territories invaded by British armies over the centuries. Little compassion or empathy had been extended towards those poorly-armed, ill-equipped peoples, who occupied that great sprawling pink swathe of the planet, whose lives had been turned upside-down by the better-armed, trinket-dispensing, resources-hungry, expansionist forces of Albion.

But this was no time for gloating. Now was the time to close ranks. Only the terminally vainglorious would be deluded enough to celebrate the fact that the house next door was on fire or that one's neighbours had been infected with TB, or that the adjoining farm had an attack of foot-and-mouth. There were some in Ireland, tragically, who were so blinded by accretions of accumulated hate that they couldn't recognise the slavering wolf loping with evil intent in the direction of their own doorstep.

Our small group had by now swelled to swarming proportions of like-minded compatriots. Now the meetings were more focused, more pragmatic. And similar groups had proliferated throughout every townland in the country. What held us all together? Not elaborate manifestos, not long-winded proclamations, but a willingness to forge a new version of Irishness, a version that was less parochial, a version that was prepared to transcend the walled-in, conditioned-reflex, anti-Britishness of the past. We were amazed and delighted at how much public opinion seemed to have changed. But had it really changed, deep down? Had the new attitudes that had surfaced always been there, like underground streams, searching for outlets, kept in their subterranean gulleys by the thou-shalt-nots of orthodox republicanism and mock-Irishry? Hundreds of thousands of Irish people had been affected by the sacrifices of their family members in World War 1, sacrifices that were dismissed, belittled, downgraded by the opinion-formers of a tunnel-visioned nationalism. 'Twas better to die 'neath an Irish sky than at Suvla or Sud-el-Bar'.....or by the Somme, or at Gallipoli, or in Kut.... went the favour-currying ballad-singers, who were always ready to jump on populist bandwagons and side with those with the easiest-to-articulate case. (Would it be only a question of time before some of them were singing pro-fascist broadsides?)

'No, it was not better to die 'neath an Irish sky', went the sub-vocalised response of very many Irish people, those who had not turned in on themselves, those who had no difficulty in acknowledging their Anglo-Irishness, a term which had been besmirched by zealots, except that to voice this reaction publicly was to risk demonisation and alienation. Sane, rational people did not wish to die unnaturally under any sky. Now the true voice of the people was being re-fashioned and it was being done in sober and reflective language. Only months previously, the Irish, shielded by a Britain prepared to stand alone in facing-up to the fascist serpent and take the flak, who were behaving like an obstreperous adolescent secure in the knowledge that while they could remonstrate and be obnoxious without restraint, that the safety-net protecting their homes and families would not be withdrawn.... All that was now changed utterly. There was now some rapid political and moral growing-up going on. The people were re-discovering a long-dormant dimension of themselves. And to acknowledge their multiple identities did not dilute, not a whit, their Irishness, no more than it made the Welsh less Welsh, the Scots less Scottish or the English less English, Geordies less Geordie, Cornish less Cornish... The ethnic spring-cleaners had done so much damage with their single-identity pogroms. Now the great national pendulum was swinging back...

A new steeliness and maturity entered the public debate. The self-pitying whine of former days was replaced by a refreshing realpolitik. The information that was coming through as a result of the lifting of the reporting on the fate of the Jews of Europe came as a bombshell to most people. People were questioning the drip-feed of anti-Judaism they had received much of it sadly through religion, from Gospel readings and sermons all through their lives, and were not any longer prepared to continue imbibing the prejudices of their forebears. The Gospels had the Jews doing this, and the Jews doing that, and what they were doing was generally none too agreeable. 'His blood be upon us and on our children', was one favourite quote, delivered with passion by clerics, for the most questionable of reasons and with blood-curdling motivations. Here were the treacherous and fickle Jews, in the Gospel accounts, welcoming Jesus on the Sunday with palms and Hosannas, but by the Friday they were baying ' Crucify him, Crucify him'. This new questioning mentality was a welcome development, which would go on into the future, I felt sure.

Ireland was now receiving a higher quality of intelligence back from Germany, stories that were beyond comprehension in their hideousness, now that Bewley had been withdrawn, and from those Jewish refugees who were getting through, thanks to people of singular virtue, like a priest in the Vatican whose name we didn't know, but whom we knew of, who was praised to the skies by the refugees, whose name, they said, would be one day honoured as one of the Righteous, by those for whom he had arranged safe passage....Stories for the future. And there were other heroes. Questions were being raised about why the Catholic Church which had known about these abuses had not let the people know about them. Thankfully, that drip-feed of anti-Jewishness that had been leached into the Irish psyche for centuries was now switched off. The architects of these hate crimes were becoming increasingly uneasy. Memories of the shabby treatment of Jews in Limerick, led by a Redemptorist priest in the early years of the century were still fresh in the public memory.

Those who had fled England in the expectation of coming back to a sleepy valley Ireland were rapidly disabused. There was no hiding place from the ominous crunch of the Nazi jackboot.

The nature of the conversation we were having about both our neighbours to the north of us and across the Irish Sea changed dramatically. Whereas in the past, whenever the North was mentioned, it was always in terms of the 'Black North', teeming with bigoted Orangemen in their bowler hats. And whenever England came up, it was always Godless, pagan England, Perfidious Albion. All this self-serving verbiage was now swept aside, replaced by 'we're-all-in-this-together', and 'we'd-better-all-hang-together-or-we'll-all-hang-separately' sentiments. Now we were talking about friends and neighbours. I found this so heartening, that a people who had been fed on a distorting diet of anti-British propaganda for so long, could in such a short space of time brush it all aside, and care so much not just about erstwhile enemies, but about vast swathes of peoples throughout Europe and further afield, people they knew so little about, had barely heard of before. The fact that they could make common cause with perfidious Albion when some nations of Europe, particularly Catholic Spain and Italy had blotted their copybook with their dalliance with Fascism, was sure proof of the underlying decency and moral soundness of the Irish people. The Ireland that would emerge from out of this convulsion would not be the priest-ridden, craw-thumping backwater which had entered into it. The heart which Yeats spoke about, the heart which, through too long a sacrifice had been turned to stone, was now pumping with a renewed effulgence.

We kept hearing of more and more embryonic resistance groups being formed in every parish in the country, north and south. They were becoming known as Forsa Cosanta Eireannach – FCE. Some very surprising people were coming forward to join: – some were ex-British soldiers; some were ex-IRA men, some current members – from both pro- and anti-Treaty factions; trade unionists; 'big and 'small' farmers; artisans; the unemployed; returnees from England who knew what was coming down the pipeline; members of the clergy, Catholic and Protestant. The people had never before been so united. There were welcome and large numbers of women joining. There were members of the Local Defence Forces and serving members of the Irish Army, the Air Corps and the Marine and Coastwatching Service. The powers-that-be were content to let this loose networking to flourish, for to try to 'organise' such a civic militia would have been to misread its function, why it had come into being. There was no friction with statutory services. Never before in the history of Ireland was there such a combined will and a sense of common purpose in evidence. This harnessing of the deep will of the people is what the 1916 leaders had presumably dreamed of, which may never have happened had the executions not taken place. What a shame the leadership so spectacularly failed to channel those energies by so spectacularly failing to trust the people and bring them on board, such was their urgency to strike before the War ended, and to strike when they thought Germany was winning? Now was different. Now there was consensus from every quarter of society, and a deep-seated determination to rise to the occasion.

What would the tactics of these groups be? Primarily, to ensure survival, preferably by the pretence of superficial compliance that masked their true objectives, a skill the Irish had perfected over the centuries, to sabotage the

Germans, with minimal injury to Irish interests, human, environmental, physical.

At a meeting in late August, it was decided that it was time for contact to be made with our fellow Resistance compatriots in England. They were styling themselves the Yeomanry for a Free England – the YFE. There were similar groupings in Wales and Scotland, the YFW and the YFS.

I volunteered to travel.

Chapter 11

Delivering butter

When I told Roisin of my plan, she burst into tears. 'I can't stand this Thomas', she sobbed. 'How on earth can you do this? To England, for goodness sake! The Germans are in England and it could be only a matter of days before they're here. Have you taken leave of your senses, man? Why you anyway? God in Heaven!'

I had never seen her so distracted.

'Why me?' I began. 'I'm heavily committed now. And why should I go? Mainly because nobody knows me. I'm young so nobody will suspect I'm up to anything. The Irish have had, and still have freedom of access to Britain since the Treaty. Tim Enright tells me that a lorry laden with butter leaves the creamery each Tuesday, headed for Birmingham. The driver is Robert Noonan. He is one of us. I've been given the name of a contact in the English Yeomanry in one of the warehouses the butter is being delivered to. It is essential that there is a personal link-up with our friends over there to share intelligence on the predicament we all find ourselves in'.

'Do you know you've got a fifth columnist in your group?" she said out of the blue.

'Do we? How do you know? Tell me more'.

'My mother was at her sodality meeting last night. They had a speaker there who is connected with a Fr Fahey. Fahey is originally from Golden, but he's now a professor in some college or other. I think he is with the Holy Ghost Order.'

'So, what did this fellow have to say?'

'Apparently this Fahey character is carried away with something he calls the 'social doctrine of Christ the King'. The fellow at the meeting kept on about Fahey's belief that the world must conform to Our Divine Lord, and not He to it.'

'What the hell does that mean?' I said. 'Search me', said Roisin. 'I don't have a doctorate in theology. Apparently this Fahey fellow is no friend of the Jews, the Freemasons, (whoever they are), or the communists, either. He seems to take a much softer line with Fascism, however, which is why one of his snoopers was at your meeting and is no doubt reporting back as we speak.'

'Our meetings are open to all', I said. 'We welcome everyone. We know only too well that there are sinister elements in Ireland who would welcome in the Germans with open arms. Nothing new there. There seems to be some bizarre tie-up between fanatical Catholicism and the political right. I wonder how that will go down with Hitler? We also know that since information has been leaking out of Germany and the occupied territories about the treatment of those who are the enemies or the scapegoats of fascists, communists, non-conformists of all kinds, out-spoken Christians, Jews, homosexuals, the disabled, the handicapped,.............the list is a long one, the overwhelming majority of the people of this and other countries know that the Third Reich is a house built on a midden. I know that my cousin who is a mongol would not survive for long in Hitler's heartless utopia. And what the Nazis are denying in Germany, they will deny here. What a pity the Fr Faheys of the world, for all their ivory-tower book-learning and priggish piety, can't see that. There are quite a few priests and other brothers and nuns who are whole-heartedly involved with us, I'm pleased to say. An end would appear to be in sight to the gallop of Fahey and his ilk and the sooner the better'.

'When my mother came back from the meeting and mentioned about Fahey's snooper, my father's ears pricked up. Fahey has form, and apparently is bitterly opposed to the IRA, which he sees as a communist conspiracy'.

'He might be right there', I muttered. 'For God sake, don't tell him I said that! Anyway, how did the story about the snooper go down?'

'How do you think? Although he has drifted away from fior-Gael rigidities of his youth, ('fierce-Gaels', he calls them), he is no communist and has no time for the clergy. He sees them as parasites of sorts – they don't do what he would consider to be an honest days work in their lives, but they live like landed gentry. They tell us lesser mortals how to live. They lay down the do's and dont's of our behaviour – right into our very beds. They're a Brahmin caste of sorts, mind-masters. My father says that Ireland is more of a caste society than a social-class based society. Except that in Ireland's inverted case, it's the priests who are the untouchables. He used to be a big advocate of James Connolly's theories, but he has given up on that simplistic, blunt instrument approach, put off by the cranks who profess to have all the answers to society's ills. If Connolly had survived 1916, he would have been all for a 1917-style Russian revolution in Ireland. He saw 1916 as merely the curtain-raiser to that bigger drama. My father gave me a copy of Robert Tressell's The Ragged-Trousered Philanthropists to read. (He always called it the Ragged-Arsed Philanthropists, the name favoured by Tressell). That opened my eyes to the inequities of society, not that I needed a book to tell me how ill-divided the world is. Were it not for the thousands who leave this country for employment in England and elsewhere, the place would be teetering on the brink of chaos, Connolly or no Connolly, because of frustration, anger and pure disillusionment. Dad says he is disgusted that drones like Fahey are free to bamboozle uneducated people and fill their minds with airy-fairy twaddle about sins and indulgences and miracles and sacramentals (whatever they are), and apparitions – don't get him started on Knock. He says that James Joyce was right about Ireland being the sow that ate its own farrow and as Sean O'Casey said, "Kathleen Mavourneen, your's is a thorny way". Anyway, we are getting far away from the pressing question of your madcap plan to go to England. Thomas, please don't go'.

'Sorry, Roisin', I said, 'I travel on Tuesday morning. We cross on the night ferry from Dun Laoghaire. We travel down through Wales by the A5, through Shropshire and arrive in Birmingham on Wednesday. We then carry out our deliveries, leave on Thursday and all being equal, I'm back on Friday.'

'All being equal', she repeated. 'What about the roadblocks and the lorry searches and the document checks?'

'They know that if they make things difficult for the delivery of essential foodstuffs like butter, the supply will dry up. I am travelling as a helper. I am not known. I doubt if any interest will be shown in me'.

'What about your parents?

'They know I am getting more and more involved in political matters', I told her, 'but I haven't told them the full story behind my trip. Please, please keep what I am telling you to yourself. I know you will.'

'Thomas, you know I will', she said. 'I'm just scared to death about how all this will end. I know that what is going to happen will happen whatever we do or don't do. I also know that if you step aside from all this, concentrate on your studies, and make something of yourself, that you'll be in a stronger position in life. Why don't you let people who can influence the future, people like Mr de Valera, get on with it. Haven't you done enough?' There was a tone of pleading in her voice.

I so badly needed to tell her I loved her, but what came out was:

'Roisin, I'm thinking of packing in school', I said.

'If you do, that's the end of us'.

No goodnight kiss.

She walked defiantly away.

Chapter 12

...shorten the road...

I helped Bob Noonan to load the lorry early the following Tuesday morning. I had taken the trouble to learn a few phrases of German over the weekend. Our languages diet at school was Latin, Irish and of course the contentious tongue of the foreigner, English. Whenever a word was uttered in Irish lessons that was an obvious borrowing from English, of which there were many, the teachers would denounce it as Bearlachas, from Bearla, English, but expressed with venom, the guttural, throat-clearing 'ch' overdone as if the mouth should be washed out after its defilement. Such was the febrile linguistic climate in which we functioned.

As we headed out on the Dublin road from Cashel, the Rock was displaying itself in all its ancient splendour, rising like a stately galleon above the morning mists of the Plains of Tipperary, majestic. We had been told as children that the Rock was originally the Divil's Bit that the devil had bitten off more than he could chew of a mountain near Templemore and spat it out in Cashel. To my thinking, it was Ireland's greatest architectural treasure. But my ardour towards The Rock wasn't universally shared. My sister, some years earlier, had taken the bus over to Cashel one very wet day to see this famed monument. When she alighted from the bus, she saw an old woman leaning over a half-door, observing the passing show. My sister asked her for directions to the Rock. By now the rain was teeming down. 'Ah, sure dat ould ting', the old crone spat, 'what would you be wanting to bodder wit dat ould relic on a day like dis for? Sure nobody is interested in dat ould yoke. Musha wouldn't you get a bit of sense for yourself and stay in out of the rain. You haven't come far, have you?' Not the salutation my naïve sister expected. To me it was the greatest monument in Ireland, magnificent, soaring, a poignant reminder of what we must have once been, and could be again. But as I said, not everyone agreed with me.

Despite the encircling gloom that was the backdrop to our journey, Bob turned out to be an excellent travelling companion, shortening the road with an engaging flow of conversation, like the Goban Saor's son. He told me about his own school days. They were expected to learn great wodges of poetry, most of which he seemed to have retained. Although he wasn't happy about some of the Brothers' approach to education, he was nevertheless a staunch defender of what they had done, not just in our town, but for the people of Ireland in general. Where would we be without those men – and those women, the Sisters of Mercy from the convent, in our town's case. Ireland can never repay the debt it owes them or to the missionaries who have spread the good name of Ireland to the back-of-beyonds of the world. He had also attended my school, the Abbey, but had to leave for reasons of family poverty. Bob said he could have taken an exam to win an Erasmus Smith scholarship but when he heard who Erasmus Smith was, and how he had acquired his wealth, he refused to have anything to do with that tainted money. Smith was an adventurer who had done well under Cromwell, and probably out of guilt, had set up schools in Tipperary, Galway and Drogheda, and a bursary that was still paying out money for scholarships, right up into our time.

Bob came out with a line I had often heard from my father, that in Ireland it wasn't what you know but who you know that was the key to personal advancement. I had already seen much favouritism at school, but I was determined not to be derailed by what I perceived to be an overly cynical attitude. A new age was about to dawn, or so I liked to tell myself.

'No, Thomas, it's not the Church's works I have a problem with', he said. 'My problem is with their pomps. But that bubble will burst in the fullness of time. Mark my words. They have gone too far in their control mania. I was talking with my wife only the other night, about the multiplicity of ways they control the people. There are Novenas, Masses, the family rosary, the Confraternity, the Legion of Mary, the Children of Mary, the Pioneers, sodalities, the sacraments, the Nine Fridays, Benediction, Pilgrimages, Indulgences, Lent, the annual Missions, prayers in schools on the hour, not to mention ejaculations. (These were short prayers said to gain indulgences). You can't have a club, be it sporting or cultural without having a Spiritual Director. They have insinuated themselves into the warp and weft of every detail of people's lives, right down to the most private. They have expropriated the language of the family - Father, Mother, Sister, Brother - in their Grand Scheme to turn the whole of society into a macro family of their designing. The people will eventually wake up to how they have been got at.

As we drove along he recited snippets of poems, songs, ballads - lines he had memorised since primary school. Despite the weighty matters that burdened me, it was pure joy listening to him. One of his favourite poems was Barbara Freitchie by John Greenleaf Whittier. We recited it together as the car sped along, both of us fighting back tears:

'Up from the meadows rich with corn,
Clear in the cool September morn
The clustered spires of Frederick stand
Greenwalled by the hills of Maryland.......

Who touches a hair of yon grey head

Dies like a dog. March on', he said....
All day long through Frederick streets
Sounded the tread of marching feet
All day long that free flag tossed
Over the heads of the rebel host...
Barbara Freitchie's work is o'er
And the rebel rides on his raids no more....
Honour to her and let a tear
Fall for her sake on Stonewall's bier
And ever above the stars look down
On the stars below in Frederick town ....'

But it wasn't Fredericksburg in verdant Maryland we had in mind as we heavy-heartedly intoned those lines, but Tipperary in the verdant Golden Vale, and all the other enslaved, and soon-to-be-enslaved Tipperarys.

On this particular early September morning there was a strange eerieness about the countryside, a pathetic fallacy of sorts, as if the land, the cattle, the birds, knew something we didn't. There was little or no movement on the roads, or in the towns - Urlingford, Johnstown, Durrow, Abbeyleix, – all deserted. As we approached Portlaoise, or Maryborough as Bob called it, the name going back to Plantation times when it was named after Bloody Mary, we finally learned why the strange stillness had descended on the countryside.

There was a roadblock outside the town; a German roadblock. They had finally arrived. I had listened to what had passed for 'news' that morning. There had been no hint that anything untoward had taken place. Yet here they were, checking all traffic, checking vehicles, checking papers.

Bob managed to let them know that we were headed to England with a consignment of best Tipperary butter. His eulogy about his cargo cut no ice with the humourless soldiery. After a cursory check they let us through. As we moved on and up through Co. Kildare there were convoys of troops, hundreds of them, it seemed, heading south.

'This is it', Bob said. 'What we have most dreaded, our worst nightmare. Just what the wing-and-a-prayer brigade said would never happen. Well it has'.

There were more roadblocks as we approached Dublin. Bob began to worry about missing the 8 o'clock sailing. We were waved through – 'Butter fur England' I kept saying in my best Teutonic brogue. I had written it out and Bob held it up. The butter was packed securely, in expertly-constructed wooden boxes, little butter coffins, which were tamper-proof.

We slept in the lorry on the ferry over. The crossing was rough. I took the opportunity to make a tour of the decks, the lounges and the bar of the ship, and was appalled to see the conditions in which my fellow countryman and women were forced to make the nightly voyage from their homeland for employment in England. I had heard of these ships being described as 'cattle boats' and the revolting state of the toilets and wash-rooms confirmed my worse forebodings. It was difficult to find a safe place to step in the toilets. The sloshings of human disgorgings and the smell were revolting. By six o'clock the following morning we were on the road out of Holyhead and headed for Birmingham. More roadblocks.

'They're crawling all over the place like ants, these Nazis', said Bob.

'Ants, Antzies', I said.

It was my first glimpse of England and Wales and my heart was downcast to see the luxuriant countryside under the cosh of these thugs. Wales looked so much like Ireland, I thought, except that the towns did appear more prosperous and better kept. North Wales was a revelation, the mountains more dramatic than the Galtees, Snowdon clearly higher than my beloved Galteemore, but not occupying the same place of affection in my heart.

We stopped for breakfast in Shrewsbury. It didn't take us long to notice that while some of the natives called the place Shroosbury, (to rhyme with shoe), others pronounced it Shrowsbury, (to rhyme with show). It was just as I imagined a charming old English market town might be, with its weather-seasoned, time-creaked, timber-framed, bockety buildings. I took careful note of everything because I knew Roisin would question me about every detail. We were no sooner parked than we had a visit from the Antzies.

'Wohin gehst du?' one said. 'Vare are you goink?" his mate echoed in English.

'To Birmingham. Butter', said Bob, gesturing the spreading of butter on bread.

'Butter? Ja? Lass mich sehen? Let me see?'

Bob prised off one of the wooden lids, and there packed with consummate precision, were 48 pounds of the best nutritious Tipperary butter, the pride of the Golden Vale.

What happened next was no surprise. Twelve boxes, from the back of the lorry were unloaded amidst great glee and we were sent on our way.

'Bastards', Bob said, as we got back on the road. 'There goes my bonus. I wangle a few boxes for myself', he tapped the side of his nose as he spoke, which I interpreted as a 'keep-that-to-yourself' gesture. 'And they are in for a double surprise when they open them. I do a sideline in poteen and there are a dozen bottles concealed in those boxes at the back. I hope they drink it fast and it poisons the shaggers'.

After a few miles on the road, when he had time to ruminate on our bad luck, Bob exploded. 'Jesus', he started, 'it's just like those other feckers on the Border. Whenever I do a delivery to Belfast or Derry, those lousers, either the IRA, or the RUC, cream off a quota for themselves. This is just like being back home. No difference. Where but in Ireland would you find the people most worked-up about the removal of the Border to be the very people who profit most from its retention? All just a bunch of parasitic Me-Feiners, the lot of them,'

The smoke clouds in the sky announced our approach to Birmingham. The city had suffered badly for the rain of bombs which had spilled down on it. Gangs of workmen were at full tilt keeping the roads open for traffic. Shells of bombed-out buildings seemed to sway drunkenly, undecided whether to retain their dignity or collapse in a heap. We arrived at Digbeth, near the city centre at around 11 o'clock and headed for the distribution warehouse. Bob knew his way around the winding streets. We were closely watched by the Antzies as the boxes were transferred to the fridges.

When we stopped for lunch, one of the men, in a heavy Brummie accent looked at me and said: 'It's a long way to Tipperary'. That was my cue to accompany him. He led me to the back of the building. He introduced himself as Ken Hughes. 'Ain't you a bit young to be involved in this sort of stuff?' he began. 'I suppose I am', I replied, 'but age is not here-nor-there in the present circumstances. I am here to tell you the Germans have arrived in Ireland and are fanning out across the country. There is a rapidly developing underground network of resistance groups in Ireland, North and South. We call ourselves the FCE – Forsa Cosanta Eireannach – the Irish Defence Force. We have the full backing of every level of Government, right up to Mr de Valera, whom I have met personally.'

'You have met de Valera?' he said, sounding surprised. 'That makes two of us. I nearly shot him in 1916. I was one of the ill-starred firing squad in Kilmainham. I was a young recruit in the British Army and was ordered to do things that have become seared into my memory and haunt my conscience, things I now wish had never happened. And particularly now that Ireland has taken the stance it has, things can now be said that would have festered until we had all died. We English handled things very badly, very badly indeed. I'm glad to say de Valera was spared, though I've never understood why''. I could tell there was much that remained to be said. 'I've read a lot since, and if I had had my way, Ireland would never have been pushed out of the Union as it was. And I mean that – pushed out. Our problem was not being able to decide what was, or was not, a colony. We seemed to believe that to be a colony it had to be far away. We kept saying that Ireland was not a colony but everything we did contradicted this piece of self-serving hypocrisy. I know that there are many who won't agree with me, but O'Connell should have been treated better. And Parnell should have been listened to. In many ways, I sympathise with those who carried out the putsch in 1916. Executing them without proper trials was wrong in every way. Even then, it should have been possible to salvage the situation and an honourable settlement arrived at. The Unionists were given too much respect and the nationalists too little. The House of Lords, that relic of an undemocratic past, should have been wound up there and then, a Norman hand-me-down that was stuffed with reactionary land-rich fossils. The Irish are not the only people to be dogged by their inability to distinguish between correlation and causation, but they have paid the heaviest of prices.'

There followed a brief silence.

'Any way Thomas', Ken said, coming out of his reverie, 'we're all in the same boat now, now that Jerry has finally arrived in your country. Do the resistance groups have a strategy to deal with the new situation?'

'We intend to follow a policy of superficial acquiescence, a form of passive resistance. What we have heard from Europe is that to confront them militarily is to invite savage and disproportionate retaliation – something we're not unfamiliar with, to our cost. The Black and Tans left their malign mark on our town. There is one location, the spot in the Hills, where they brutally did to death the young man Michael Edmunds, still regarded with reverence by the people of the town.There's no alternative at the moment but to behave with circumspection with these gentlemen. We intend to box clever and to keep our powder dry. We hope to lull them into a false sense of security by offering a front of fake civility. They react with excessive viciousness when crossed. So we have decided to learn from the old Russian tactic that outfoxed Napoleon, draw them in, lull them into a false sense of security, and when the time comes, let them have it. Because of the stance taken by the Irish in the past with regard to Germany, they think that we will be a push-over. They mistakenly think that they are home and dry in Irish affections, but the Irish will not fall for their wiles.'

'It's so good to hear what you have to say. I shall let comrades up and down this country and also in Wales and Scotland know that we are all singing from the same hymn-sheet. There will be other contacts between the populations, but this is the first I know of. I was very disappointed when Ireland declared for neutrality. Part of me sort of understood, considering our appalling treatment of the Irish in the past. But when a monster like Hitler stalks the horizon, it's time for old enmities to be put on the back burner and for common cause to become the priority. This particular snake needs beheading. We were overjoyed here to hear Mr de

Valera's speech on St Patrick's Day. He must have been very well advised by someone', said Ken.

'He must have been', I replied.

And left it at that.

Chapter 13

...the Antzies crawl...

The Antzies were crawling all over my town when we got back - in the Spittal, in the New Town, in the Market Yard, in Coolnagun and Garnacanty and everywhere else. They seemed to be all over the place, trying to ingratiate themselves with the 'natives', especially the women. Forces of occupation put women in a very difficult predicament. Women throughout history have fallen foul of nationalist ideologues, many of whom themselves were fanatical and emotionless psychopaths who had only a glimmer of understanding of the workings of the human heart, or the gut, for that matter. Fortunately for humanity, people continue to fall in love, across all man-made boundaries, and always will.

Roisin was overjoyed to have me back. She sobbed with relief when we were alone and the passion of her embraces almost frightened me. I felt a new sense of responsibility for the stewardship of these feelings, a force that was overwhelming, a responsibility I knew I must not fail to cultivate, to protect and above all, not to exploit. Roisin knew, and I knew, what we both so ardently desired to do, both to and with each other, but we also knew other things. Had I crossed that threshold, I could easily have taken advantage of that distraught girl. I'm glad I didn't. I could understand why people threw all caution to the wind at times of great upheaval, when pressures were intense, and normal standards seemed not to apply. There were times when it felt like an epiphany of sorts, when it felt that Roisin and I transmigrated one into the other, as if we swapped premises, and climbed into each other's souls. I couldn't believe that the sex which we were postponing, could ever be more powerful, or more elevating, as these rapturous, ecstatic feelings.

'Have you decided about school?' she asked, when we had returned to a plane that bore some semblance of normalcy.

'I'd better knuckle down and get the Leaving Cert out of the way', I said. I could see tears of relief coursing down her face. Roisin knew she was the author of this change of direction.

'Thank you, Thomas', she said, 'and now perhaps you'll tell me how you got on in England? I can't believe you've actually been over there. What is it like? I bet you saw some nice English girls'.

If I had, now was not the time to tell Roisin. I told her about Shrewsbury and how the River Severn meandered through it, and about the Shakesperean half-timbered houses, and the medieval street plan; about how Charles Darwin had been born there; about the Roman ruins at Wroxeter, which was known back then as Viroconium the 'city of the werewolf', about how it became the settlement of the Celtic tribe, the Cornovii. I told her of our visit to the beautiful Ironbridge, built by Abraham Darby in 1779, and that when the swarming Antzies were a bad memory, we'd go there on holiday. (I nearly said 'on our honeymoon' but I decided not). In my short sojourn through Shropshire, I had fallen in love with that tranquil county, which reminded me so much of my own dear Tipperary.

I told her of the roadblocks and the look of grim sufferance and defiance on the people's faces, a look the soldier in Viroconium would have seen on the faces of the locals back nearly two thousand years ago, indeed the look that invading British soldiers had seen on the faces of natives the world over – that of superficial acquiescence veiling a passive/aggressive sullenness.

My FCE colleagues back home were very interested to hear how I had got on with the representative of the Yeomanry. They were proud to know that the German occupation had created a level playing field among the 'home nations' in what was known in the old Napoleonic ballad as the Bonny Bunch of Roses...which contained the line, '...England, Ireland, Scotland, their unity will ne'er be broke....'

People of the Bonny Bunch knew that when the fascist yoke had been cast off, a new phase of mutual respect among the citizens of the British/Irish archipelago would come into being. But that was for the future. The task for now was to lock the Germans in to consolidating their hold on the Islands by giving the appearance of us going along with their grandiose schemes. One of the first was an elaborate plan to construct motorways the length and breadth of the islands, like the autobahns that had criss-crossed Germany, a scheme like that of an earlier conqueror, the Romans, who had also expended such energy in road-building and grandiose structures. Hitler's supporters never tired in pointing out how a robust transport network had been central to copper-fastening the Nazi stranglehold on power. They were also ever-ready to point out that Herr Hitler had been elected, therefore.... Therefore nothing! All that sham election went to prove was that dictators believe in one man, one vote.....once. How democratic was the Night of the Long Knives in June and July in 1934, when that 'personification of rectitude' had the leaders of the SA (Sturmabteilung) massacred, to mention but one of his many overkills?

Thousands of workers from Europe were arriving, and work commenced on a dizzying abundance of projects. All through 1942 and '43 people marvelled at the rapid rate of progress. Even the bitterest foes of fascism had to admit that these people were awesomely efficient. There had been a previous, native example of this ability to undertake large-scale projects in the Ardnacrusha Hydroelectric scheme which had been executed by the German firm Siemans-Schuckert in 1929, a mere 7 years after independence. Of course, Irish engineers and labour were also involved and essential to the success of this mammoth project.

Not a person in the country was unemployed. Even the halt and the lame were euphemistically 'encouraged' to work, - or given the option of starving.

Teams of data-collectors combed the country, cataloguing, collating, evaluating and recording. Such a data-base as this had never been amassed about Ireland – or about Britain, since the time of the Domesday Book. The German so-called scholars who had worked in Ireland in the 1930s had already collected reams of information about all aspects of Irish society. They may have camouflaged their true interests by pretending to be folklorists, language students, Celtic Studies enthusiasts, music and dance collectors, but that was largely a front. They may, of course, have been tangentially interested in these things, but they were far more interested in building dossiers on many other areas of Irish topography and society. Hundreds of them had worked in Irish government salaried positions but, as many who worked with them suspected, they owed their first allegiance to the Fuhrer. There were even reports of Nazi gatherings under the fluttering folds of the Swastika, with Heil Hitler salutes. Some of their festivities took place in the Gresham Hotel, no less! The Irish, of course were very familiar with the existence of strata within their own upper castes which showed their first allegiance to a foreign power, Rome being one such.

As the sands of 1943 trickled down, and These Islands seemed to be, if not pacified, at least falling into line,

Hitler turned his attentions on Russia. It was always just a matter of time before the inevitable clash of ideologies had to be faced-up-to. Stalin was as interested as ever in getting his hands on Poland and Eastern Europe, and with Italy and Germany extending their empires in Africa, Hitler reckoned the time was right to launch his assault on Russia. With Russia defeated, the Third Reich would be consolidated from Valencia Island to Vladivostock. National Socialism would become the world's dominant political ideology. Communism and Soviet pretensions would be expunged from the face of the earth. Likewise the British Empire would be consigned to the history books. Hitler's 1000 Year Reich was here to stay.

The German authorities in Ireland had been given strict instructions to stay onside with the Irish. Any jobs-worth who threw his weight about was to be summarily dealt with.

A great flurry of anticipation was created when the General der Wehrmacht in January '42 asked to address the town's urban district council. Rumour was rife as to what was in the offing. We knew that there would be initiatives to communicate officially with the locals and this was the first. The Council Chamber was full to overflowing that evening. As a mark of respect to the powers-that-be the Council had agreed to permit a blood-red, long flowing Swastika to be draped down the wall of the Chamber, much to the fury and maddening displeasure of most councillors.

In every house and pub in the town, the people awaited the outcome of the meeting.

Chapter 14

... a Phoenix rises...

'Rebuild the WHAT? You can't be serious!!! Jesus, Mary and holy Saint Joseph, I never heard the like? He said WHAT?? That they were going to rebuild the BARRACKS??'

The town's Military Barracks, built by the British, had been the architectural masterpiece of the district, the Jewel in the Town, give or take a couple of churches. Built by a Victorian caste of master builders, the Barracks was a rugged, limestone entity, built to last. In fact the builders intended it to be around for a long, long time. It had lofty ceilings, with vents eight feet up, a feature which gave rise to the legend that it was originally intended for India, but there was an alleged mix-up of plans in London, and whatever was intended for Tipperary, wound up adorning the sub-continent, and vice versa. Or so the story went.

There was accommodation for about 5000 troops, and it was rumoured that in the build-up to World War 1, as many as 10,000 lambs to the slaughter were crammed in, for a crash course in how to be mown down, having taken as many lives as possible yourself, in readiness for shipment to the Front. Locals told of hearing the troops singing It's a Long Way To Tipperary as they tramped their way to the railway station, most never to see Tipperary, or their own homes, again. A very long way!

When the Barracks were built in the 1870s, they were a splendid sight as old photographs indicate. Who could have told, back then that they would prove to be a Titanic of sorts. Built for 500 years, they lasted less than 50. So, what happened?

The Barracks were to stamp an identity on the town that some resented, and resented passionately. The district had a reputation for non-conformity with the status quo, so it seemed like a very good idea to plonk a massive garrison right in the centre of the badlands, to encourage law and order. The nickname Tipperary Stonethrowers was not coined in a vacuum.

Of course, back then, in late Victorian times, headline-grabbing events such as World War 1, the Easter Rising, the Solohead Ambush, the War of Independence, the Civil War, were on nobody's agenda, but the best laid plans of mice and men..... All of those things did come to pass, throwing the plans of the Empire builders off kilter. The Barracks became an interrogation centre for political subversives, and no love was lost between the IRA and those whom they saw as Crown Forces of Occupation. The locals could never quite decide how 'occupied' they were. The word suited the ideologues but to those who supplied the needs of those hungry 'forces of occupation', it was a lucrative occupancy. In the early decades of the life of the Barracks, the locals looked benignly on the intrusion because of the economic benefits they brought to the town but when serious conflict arose during and after wartime, and particularly after three members of the Tipperary Brigade of the IRA were executed in the Barracks, all changed - changed utterly.

The downward spiral of internecine bloodletting that the Civil War, when it came, visited on the town, reached a nadir during those troubled years. (Why they are called Civil Wars, I could never fathom as I could see nothing civil about them.) The town was hopelessly divided. The anti-Treaty forces of de Valera despite losing, narrowly, the democratic vote in the Dail which ratified the Treaty, took it upon themselves to pursue by violence what they deemed to be their constitutional entitlement. The bulk of the people of Tipperary while not overjoyed by the Treaty were relieved to be at peace, and were prepared to go along with it. The British marched out of the Barracks in early 1922, and vacated the twenty six counties of the Free State. The story was told that as they mounted the ships at Kingstown, they were jeered and spat at by the Dublin rabble and unceremoniously and inhospitably sent on their way. One of the soldiers, responding to baying locals who were telling him where to go in earthy Dublinese, referred to the fact that the Normans were encouraged to come to Ireland and given the green light to arrive in 1169 by Dermot MacMurrough, turned on the mob and said: 'We were invited, you know', before scurrying up the gangplank.

What had happened in the intervening 750-plus years was the problem. Attitudes in town and district were now mortally sundered. The 'hard men', an intractable breed, the 'all-or-nothing' anti-Treaty brigade went to war. What they hoped to achieve, whether from Dublin, from Belfast, or from London, was never spelled out. If they thought that by killing old comrades and causing mayhem, the Unionists were going to have a change of heart, or the flint-hearted obdurates in London were going to throw in the towel, they were sadly mistaken. Tragically for Ireland, it has a penchant for producing, in every generation, zealots who by the spilling of blood, think they could 'free Ireland', or 'free Ulster'. They never seem to get around to letting the rest of us know precisely what their idea of 'freedom' meant. One would get the impression from reading some of the utterances of the more extreme factions, that they'd be happy only if Ireland could be towed out somewhere into the centre of the Atlantic, as far away from detested England as it was possible to get, while the others wanted to tow it in the completely opposite direction and anchor it firmly on to what they trustingly, and perhaps a tad naively call 'the mainland'.

The excesses of these extremists, who would only settle for the whole package, no compromises/no surrender, for whom political dogma trumped plain common sense, left the general populace to have to live with the messy aftermath of their unbending absolutism.

The die-hards took possession of the Barracks after the departure of the British in 1922, but were routed by pro-Treaty forces. Rather than vacate the buildings, they decided to burn down the main blocks, destroying hundreds of thousands of pounds worth of property, which could have been key to the future economic life of the town. This perverse action, in their minds, killed many birds with one stone, it cleansed the town of reminders of British occupation, it deprived the Free State forces of occupancy of the Barracks, it exacted a revenge of sorts on the now non-existent British occupiers. Whatever their motives most of the fine old buildings, swallowed by flames, lay in ruins. Barrels of paraffin were spilt on the fine woodwork, flames leaped into the heavens and the conflagration, like a funeral pyre, was reportedly seen for miles around. The skeletal remains of the erstwhile gleaming military premises now haunted the town. The people were stunned into silence at the enormity of the crime. They were terrified to say or do anything in protest, for the perpetrators of that act of gross vandalism probably walked among them and were probably still armed. I asked questions of my parents and others, but the code of omerta was as alive-and-well in our town as ever it was among Mafia networks in Southern Italy. The old photographs of those rugged limestone buildings would still give me a pang, for had the hand of the arsonist been stayed, Tipperary might well have been the headquarters of the Irish Army of the new Free State, or at least the location of the Southern Command of that army. Or who knows, a University, even an expanded Abbey School? But the buildings were gutted, the people of the town were gutted, the town itself was gutted.

When word went round that the Germans, having had their surveyors to examine the charred shells of the buildings, decided that most of them were solid and salvageable, the reaction in the town was one of restrained exultation. 'If they are prepared to make a gift of those buildings to us, the second time they will have been so gifted, there'll be no looking of gift horses in the mouth'... was the general consensus.

But there was a problem. A member of the public, a tall, gaunt man, with a commanding presence and a slight stammer, stood up. He was a regular attendee at our FCE meetings. 'I represent the people of Glenview Square', he began. 'We rent the 36 houses which the Council has refurbished on the Barracks site. How can we live in the midst of such military goings-on? We oppose this initiative'.

Gasps of disbelief went round the council chamber. The German General stood up and spoke. 'We have anticipated this objection. These families cannot be expected to tolerate a foreign soldiery on their doorsteps. We propose to offer these people newly-built, modern, three and four bedroom houses in Scallagheen. They will have hot and cold running water, bathrooms and generous gardens. The residents will own these houses outright, and will be given freehold papers to that effect. We have already bought the land. We shall station our own personnel in Glenview Square, which from henceforth will be known as Mein Kampfstrasse'. From Glenview Square, or Radharc an Ghleanna, in the Irish language, to this verbal monstrosity would have been a deal-breaker in normal times.

The Glenview spokesman was speechless. The Councillors were speechless. There was no gratitude expressed. Not only was it an offer we could not refuse, it was an offer we dare not refuse. The meeting concluded.

Every builder, bricklayer, plasterer, carpenter, plumber, painter and decorator, and labourer for miles around piled into the town. One often heard those working on the refurbishment recall that their grandparents or other relatives had worked on the original Barracks in the late 1870s. They felt a similar sense of proprietorship about those cherished buildings as artisans of earlier times had felt as generation after generation of their families worked on the cathedrals, handing on their skills. When a great edifice becomes part of the physical backdrop of people's lives, its loss or destruction leaves a sense of permanent bereavement. This was often said of the shipbuilders of Belfast after the loss of the Titanic, when all that expertise and attention to detail were swallowed, in that case, by the deep. In this case the flames had done the consuming. The fires raging in the hearts of a few had spread to the non-partisan fabric of the Barracks.

Work proceeded apace, and by mid-1944 the Barracks were the headquarters of the Heer, the army division of the Wehrmacht. The Germans couldn't understand why the townspeople had thrown their energies so enthusiastically into re-creating what had been the headquarters of the British of unlamented memory. But Tipperary people are deep. They would be the last people on earth to divulge to these most recent forces of occupation, their reasons for being enthusiastic in regenerating such an iconic part of the fabric of their town, after its criminal violation, whatever the back-story.

The local Brass and Reed Band, which had prudently declined invitations to participate in public events since the German arrival, claiming prior commitments, grasped the opportunity to lead the parade the day the Barracks were reopened. Down the Main Street, the familiar and well-loved strains of Knocknagow and Slievenamon filled the people's hearts to overflowing, with cross-currents of emotion, nostalgia, pride, fury, determination, the depths of which the grinning Antzies could never have dreamed of. They were shut out from such private concealments. Then, as the Band was passing the statue of Charles J Kickham, that revered old patriot in the homes of Tipperary, the order was given by the bandmaster, to listen for the double-tap of the drums, to slow down and mark time. The band then struck up a well-loved favourite, Old Comrades. This old marching tune, which hailed originally from Germany, had been bequeathed to the Band by the now departed and much respected British bandmaster of the old Barracks and it had become a standard among the people of the town. The Germans thought, of course, that it was being played as a tribute to them. They knew it as Alte Kamaraden. But it most emphatically wasn't being played for them. It was being played for and to our own people; for all those who, down the years had loved our town and our country with an undimmed devotion; it was being played for all those, both present and absent, near and far, now and in the past, who had played their part in keeping the banner of nobility and self-belief raised aloft, in other dark days. It was being played for the sons and daughters of the town who had strayed far from home to share the good name of Tipperary with the world. And these, despite outward appearances, with red Swastika flags draped from bank and cinema and council buildings, were dark days indeed. As the Band continued on its way along Main Street, past the Maid of Erin monument, erected to honour the Manchester Martyrs, Allan, Larkin and O'Brien, and up Davitt Street, it struck up Tipperary's Hills for Me, followed by It's a Long Way to Tipperary, a cheer from the heart from all those lining the streets, a cheer that mystified the gaping Germans, a cry from the very soul of the townspeople, a people who had behaved with such forbearance, such dignity, such self-discipline during the last few years, rent the air. But their ability to demonstrate such control and forbearance was neither begged, nor borrowed, nor stolen. It was serenely acquired over many a year. As the Band passed along, through the New Town, scene of tumult during the Rent and Land Wars of bygone days, the crowds joined in behind it, until the town's streets were thronged. Then back to the band-room after an historic outing. There had never before been witnessed such a demonstration of dignity, loyalty and determination in our town.

The press photos of the new Barracks looked like a reincarnation of the old – as if new life had been breathed into old bones, a Lazarus come back to us. The sight of the Swastika, where the Union Jack once fluttered, flying over the square was probably the hardest thing of all for the locals to stomach.

As 1944 guttered to an end, a pattern of sorts had established itself. The old chapel had been re-consecrated as a Lutheran church and many of the other soldiers had achieved a level of integration of sorts, turning up to mass in the parish church, many of them being Catholics from Bavaria. They sat together, dutifully paying their thrupenny bits which entitled people to process down the central aisle of the church, seats occupied by the middle castes of the town, to which was now added another caste, that of Nazi storm-trooper. Nobody was quite sure yet where exactly in the pyramid these new arrivals fitted in. We just knew they were in there, cuckoo-like. As 1944 drew to a close, those locals who had found employment in the Barracks, in the kitchens, or the laundries, or the gardens, or in maintenance, reported that troop numbers in the canteens, and in the dormitories and on the parade grounds, were quite noticeable dropping.

Where could they be going?

We were living in a news vacuum. The BBC, as it had been, was no more. Not as a credible source of news, at any rate. Radio Eireann was striving manfully, under the baleful eye of the Nazi authorities, to keep people's spirits up, but there was a limit to what could be expected from a diet of musics, traditional and Classical and Delia Murphy's inimitable singing. Songs like If I were a Blackbird, The Croppy Boy, Down By The Glenside, took on a new and deeper significance. They were a link with something precious and authentic. There was no jazz, which the Germans – officially – deemed to be degenerate, but which they listened to avidly, hypocrites that they were. But as far as news was concerned....

We in the FCE continued to meet whenever possible under multiple guises, sporting, cultural, and recreational. Hurling and football matches were an opportunity for FCE compatriots in other parishes to have an excuse to come to our town and exchange notes. I missed many a meeting which was being held on the sidelines, while Arravale Rovers were seen to slog it out against Lattin-Cullen or the Galtee Rovers, with me, on the pitch, trying to score the odd point.

We had a visitor at one of our meetings in January 1945. He was a young man, not very much older than me. He had come to my house and said he had been sent by Ken in Birmingham. I shook his hand and waited for him to speak. 'It's a long way to Tipperary', he said in an unmistakeable French accent.

Chapter 15

...benedictus qui venit...

His name was Benedict. He was a member of the Maquis. He came from Hurigny, a hamlet near Macon in the Saone valley. He had travelled extensively throughout Europe and was a fund of information on how the ebb and flow of war was steeling the resolve of millions to slay the dragon of fascism. He had travelled by fishing boat from the Welsh coast to Curracloe in Wexford, from whence he was spirited by compatriots to Tipp. He was based in London and was one of a network of hundreds of thousands who were waiting vigilantly, biding their time, waiting for the moment to strike. It seemed that that time was fast approaching.

He told us that the German incursion into Russia, which was now well advanced, was leeching the might and heft of the Wehrmacht, sucking it into the very vacuuming maw of the Soviet Union. He informed us that the Russians, in an almost carbon copy of the Napoleonic campaign, kept falling back, falling back, laying waste their own land. He carried fraternal greetings from resistance groups throughout Europe and further afield to the noble people of Ireland for dealing so skilfully with the Nazis or Antzies as the Irish call them so wittily, a label which had gone far afield. He said that what has happened in Germany and in the occupied territories is too hideous to even begin to go into. All will be revealed in the fullness of time when the camps are liberated, some of which were being so as we speak.

'Do you have any questions?'

Nearly everyone there raised a hand.

'Why did Russia sign the Molotov/Ribbentrop Pact in the first place?'

'Historians will analyse this bizarre agreement, if agreement it can be called. It was shameful from the Russian point of view and had to do with the carve-up of Eastern Europe, of Poland and the Baltic States, of Finland, Romania, the so-called 'spheres of influence'. Russia claimed to be worried about what it expediently called 'capitalist encirclement'. The Pact had the aspect about it of two rabid dogs encircling each, sniffing each other before a fight, each equally in mortal dread of the other. These warlords, Hitler and Stalin are no different from any other empire-builders or land-grabbers of the past, Genghis Khan, Alexander the Great, William the Conqueror, Napoleon, Oliver Cromwell......and all the rest. The true story of American, Australian and many other expansionist sagas has yet to be told. It's a long list. And a banal story, but truth will out. Gone are the days when the conquerors and their lackey 'historians' got away with telling a pack of lies'.

It was clear that Benedict knew his history. He was saying things that resonated with us.

'And why did the Pact come to an end?'

'Well the National Socialists in Germany, and the Socialist Socialists, or Communists, as they style themselves, in Russia, were both vehemently anti-capitalist, both having designs on eventually extending their ideological empires right across the entire globe. Both considered that the very recent past was the most auspicious time to strike, while the iron was hot, and were prepared to stop at nothing in the global chess game that was shaping up in the 30s. It was a brutal game. Life counted for little in the eyes of these monsters and not just human life - all life.' (He spoke the last words with a grave emphasis.)

'What do those psychopaths care about the environment or those defenceless life forms that depended on it for their survival? Talks had begun between Britain, France and Russia in August 1939, but Stalin's demands could not be met, particularly with regard to Poland. But it was the so-called Operation Barbarossa on June 27 1941 when Hitler attacked Soviet positions in Eastern Poland that finally brought the Pact down.'

'What do the people of Eastern Europe think of the German occupation?'

'German people as yet unborn will never live down the evils and excesses of Nazism. The Reich which Hitler tried to bring into existence is grossly unsustainable and when it disintegrates, men, women and children of goodwill the world over will say 'Good Riddance'. Any ideology that has both supremacism and hate, simultaneously at its core, is of its very nature short-lived.'

'Why did the Germans go easier on Western Europe, including us in these islands, since they arrived?'

'I believe that the order went out from the German High Command - the diktat known as 'Bauen und befreunden' - 'Build and Befriend' - was designed to consolidate their position in occupied territories. They realised that by antagonising the conquered peoples, massive resources would be required to put down rebellions. England was the keystone. When that was down, the need for savage repression diminished. Hence the softly, softly approach. Your local project to rebuild the Barracks is one example of this policy. Have you noticed the Arbeit Macht Frei ironwork installed over the gates of the refurbished Barracks? It was one of the first things I spotted. It is also to be seen at the entrances to hell-holes like Dachau, outside Munich, and at Auschwitz/Birkenau in southern Poland, death swamps that will cause people to recoil in horror for as long as human memory survives. When those who liberate those god-forsaken places see what is to be seen, many of them will never recover. When the naïve advocates of neutrality, and not just around here, were trying to convince themselves and the world that what was going on in Europe was 'none of our business' they were whistling in the dark. What is going on in places like Dachau concerns all people with even a tenuous claim to belonging to the human family. There are no non-combatants in the battle between fascism and freedom. In my country the names Vichy and Petain will live in ignominy. We should be grateful for clear thinkers like Churchill, for all his other blind spots, who had the measure of Hitler before anyone else, as far as I'm concerned. There are also massive projects being undertaken by the Germans throughout these islands, including an elaborate scheme to repair the damage done to London and southern England. It's a ruse to use the returning soldiery as semi-slave labour, both providing employment and distracting them at one fell swoop. I've even heard in my travels that there's a plan in the pipeline to, wait for it, re-roof the Rock of Cashel and bring it back into use. Maybe it'll be Hitler's Irish Berchtesgaden, from which he can lord it over all he surveys like an ancient king of Munster?' Jaws dropped and eyes popped when we heard this outlandish story.

'Another reason for the kid-glove tactics is to lull people into a false sense of security. Make no mistake these people are vile, treacherous bastards.' (The use of such strong language from such a mild-spoken man had an added punch). 'If you think the Brits were arrogant, you've witnessed nothing yet. It's a welcome development that the Irish people are waking-up to what fascism really means, but hopefully, for you, events in Eastern Europe will forestall the Irish having to experience the full savagery of what these sinister fiends have in store for you. If Hitler isn't stopped, by 1950, there will not be a Jew, a handicapped person, physically or mentally, a homosexual, or a communist, in these parts. You don't have Jehovah's Witnesses around here, but if you had, they will be gone too. In Europe there are extermination camps in which unspeakable things are happening. I've heard of a doctor called Mengele in one of those camps and when it is revealed what sinister experimentation he's been up to, people will struggle to believe it. When we hear of such evils, we tend to question them and to doubt the messenger, as someone who is hopelessly prejudiced, a fantasist, an exaggerator, that the reality couldn't be that bad. Believe me, it's a lot worse. Hitler is a crazed lunatic and probably a drug addict, if rumours are to be believed. No sane person could be presiding over what he is authorising, and allowing it. He thinks that, as well as the Jews, that coloured and Asian people are subhuman. I'm not entirely certain what he thinks in his heart-of-hearts about you Irish. I dread to think what the population of the world will look like in 1970 unless a stop is put to his gallop. Those who argued for neutrality will have had a rude awakening, their arguments swept aside by a tidal wave of evil. There have been attempts to assassinate Hitler, but by fanatics who are more extreme than himself.

It is my belief that Mr de Valera and his cabinet have been removed into one of those places of incarceration, along with Mr Churchill and his cabinet. My sources tell me that the British Royal family are also confined there. I've heard that Colditz is the name of the prison. That goon of a stooge Edward VIII and his fancy woman, Mrs Simpson are reinstated......for now.

But to finish the answer to your question, the main reason for the change of emphasis is, I believe, for the Germans to create time and space to build the atomic bomb. With the British out of the game, and the Russians under siege, Hitler knows that if he beats the Americans to that most prized of goals, he will truly rule the world.'

'How far advanced are his plans?'

'Nobody knows for sure, but there are reliable sources which it would be very foolish to dismiss. The Germans are also perfecting ballistic missiles with a range of about 1000 kilometres, 600 miles. There's an aerospace genius called Wernher Von Braun who is behind this advanced rocketry. He was well known in the 1930s so we are sure he is behind the V2 rocket'.

'Why are you telling us all this?'

'Because this was the first group of its kind in Ireland; people throughout Europe know of you. It was from this modest seed that a vast network has spread throughout this country. It will not be possible to mount a convincing argument against the unification of Ireland when the war is over. Those clinging to the wreckage of the past had better climb on to terra firma, and not just in Ireland. The Germans have brazenly and falsely claimed to have 'unified' the country, trying to curry favour with some flaky types. Proper, agreed unification will follow, and can only follow, the departure of the Nazis.

The unreal stalemate we have lived through will come to an abrupt end during the spring of 1945. The plan is for the Russians and the Americans to scythe their way through the remnants of the Wehrmacht by April 25th. The meeting point is to be Torgau on the Danube. A vast army from India, China, and Africa are poised to strike at the head of the snake.

'What can we do?'

'What you have been doing is an inspiration to us all. We have used a variety of tactics to frustrate the Germans, to halt their trains, to compromise their plans, to put their installations out of commission. You in Ireland, have a world reputation for the production of 'home-made' explosives of all kinds. Lay in stores of such ordnance in case they are needed, and hope they won't be. Once the German collapse in Eastern Europe begins to bite, I doubt if they will put up much of a fight so far from home, in places like this.

One easy-to-manufacture device which has proven invaluable to us in France, which I don't think has been used in Ireland, is to choose biggish lumps of house coal. Drill a hole in them. Pack the hole with dynamite, seal the hole with a core of coal. Whenever we wish to stop a train carrying weaponry, tanks, vehicles, building materials, or frustrate a meeting of a local high command, we strategically drop some of these coal-bombs into the coal carts, or we 'arrange' to have them added to the coal supplies for an installation, destroying furnaces, boilers, heating systems. We have even had our own people doing the shovelling and jumping clear before the bang. Consternation is caused when these unidentifiable devices do their work; keeps the enemy in a state of constant insecurity. Fortunately you haven't had to wage that sort of campaign. And I hope you never do'.

We got to work on stockpiles anyway. Just in case. We had some experts in our ranks who had a long history of dealing in such makeshift devices.

Chapter 16

…a strained stalemate…

Roisin was at University. Although there was no tradition in her family of higher education, not to mention medicine, she was determined to be a doctor. That was a brave choice in the Ireland of that time because women were presented with very narrow options. Had she gone for teaching, or secretarial work, or being a nun, no questions would have been asked. But doctoring? Neighbours were saying she had notions, or figaries (which rhymed with canaries), above her station. The people who went on for medical studies in our town were for the most part children of doctors, or other professional types. I could never quite work this out myself. Was it that these propensities were handed on genetically, or that the children of doctors grew up devoid of the mystique of medicine, which like religion, was seen in cultic terms? Doctors were looked-up-to as wonder-workers. If we of the lower orders wished to see the doctor, we had to queue up at the Dispensary, armed with our Medical Cards, (if we were fortunate enough to have one). The Dispensary was housed in the old Workhouse buildings. The doctor, would breeze in, usually late, as if he were a member of a higher caste. The doctors and the chemists always seemed to be so well-fed looking, so unlike the great unwashed, the neglected souls who queued-up to see them. The seats were long benches, which we called forms, pronounced 'furrums', and people shuffled along the furrum, to be next in to see the doctor. The system was not unlike confessions, where you joined the queue for a spiritual top-up. Here you hopefully got a medical one.

The doctor always asked you to open your mouth, and say AAAGGGHH!, then he - always a he - would pull down your lower eye skin flap to see if you were anaemic, in which case a bottle of Parish's Food was the solution – you could almost see the iron filings suspended in the red liquid. It tasted ghastly and stained your teeth black. These procedures, the tongue and the eye, were performed whatever your symptoms. He rushed you through the consultation because of the milling crowd outside, scribbling a prescription for the chemist. It was a miracle that people weren't poisoned from the wrong potions because the doctor's scrawl was completely illegible – another way of keeping the plebs in the dark, I thought. There was but a wavy line on many of those prescriptions, which on occasion caused to chemist to go over into the doctor to ask him for clarification. People's hearts thumped in their chests when they went into that surgery. The doctor must have thought that most people in the town had cardiac arrhythmia because of the anxious pounding of people's fearful hearts as they appeared before him.

It also intrigued me that the chemist, in a smallish room with limited shelving always seemed to have the correct medicines for the many ailments that the doctor diagnosed. His shuttered hatch reminded me of the confessional, or of the apertures through which mendicants received alms in medieval times, the giving hand always above the receiving one, which we were never allowed to forget. The slot was about one foot square, and people could barely see the chemist, the opening being so restricted. The profusion of Thank Yous, kow-towings, and head-bowings, which were offered to the medical staffs, to doctor, chemist and nurse, like religious mantras, were a symptom of how much the people had to abase themselves before these powerful people. And like the priests, they gave the impression that they saw such demeanings as their due entitlement, the natural law of the way things are and they should be, and would continue to be, if they had any say in the matter. So much for the New Broom of Freedom!

Of course, only those who were near destitute turned up at the Dispensary. If a person had to see the doctor urgently, outside of Dispensary hours, an appointment had to be made, and either the doctor came to the house or we had to go to their houses. This entailed the incurring of serious expense, because these august people were not charities. Their children's fees at expensive schools had to be paid, after all. And a private education didn't come cheap. Many a death, young and old, was the consequence of delayed interventions by doctors, brought on by parents crippled by worry about lack of money.

One often heard people in the chemist shops, in an attempt to avoid paying a doctor's fee, describing symptoms to the chemist, publicly, in that public place, with other customers standing round listening. This was degrading, but such was the desperation people lived with, that they had no choice but to put up with it. I had read somewhere of a Report in England called the Beveridge Report that promised health and welfare services...

One day I was in the chemist shop to buy plasters when a woman was describing a back pain her husband was suffering. She went into great detail, to the bemusement and embarrassment of the other shoppers, pretending not to hear, as the chemist listened intently. He eventually disappeared behind the magic door, like a medieval alchemist, to where the potions were concocted, to emerge some minutes later with a tiny, shiny, circular red cardboard box containing ointment.

He gave it to the poor woman and told her to tell her husband to rub it in well. 'How much do I owe you, Mr Kinsella?' she asked. '£5', he said, 'and it's important that he rubs it in well'. Her jaw dropped when she heard the exorbitant cost of the unguent. That was a week's wages. 'OK Sir' she repeated, '£5 and rub it in well. And you're not doing so bad a job yourself, Mr Kinsella', she said giving him a steely stare and regretting ever having come near him, as the other customers stifled their laughter.

Roisin was determined to fight against these humiliations and I was proud of her for being so determined. When it became known in the town that she was aiming for medicine, there was no contact from the medical caste, either encouraging or welcoming her. One could almost sense the lack of enthusiasm that someone from a lower caste was deigning to break through an invisible sheath. It was clear that nothing much had changed since the British left Ireland, all the old ingrained habits and practices were still there. In some ways they were worse, the pecking orders were, if anything, more entrenched and annoying now, that it was our own looking down on their own. The hierarchies in our town were suffocating. It never ceased to fascinate me how the sands of privilege seemed to have closed over, and the new upper castes so seamlessly had taken over the mantle of top dog and had so effortlessly taken to lording it over the same old masses. Sometimes I wondered if the priests and the doctors and the lawyers, the Brahmin caste, and easily the worst offenders, got together in secret enclave to discuss how to perfect the art of keeping the hoi polloi in their place. I knew they didn't, and yet I marvelled at how the structures of social control so naturally perpetuated themselves. Was it, as was often pointed out by the anti-British brigade, a mentality of subservience, the 'slave mind' that was bred into the people over centuries of oppression, or was it a more home-grown phenomenon, a residue of the clan system, still an inhibiting force in our society, but unacknowledged. If anything, the sentimental voices of nationalism were more inclined to look back to the 'old pre-British, pre 1600, order' with nostalgia. I was veering towards the latter theory, not as a total explanation of our hierarchies, as I saw how each of the strata of society kept themselves unto themselves and how the subtle ancient forces of control were still strong, aided and abetted by a conditioned social sycophancy.

Because of the tumultuous history of land forfeiture and even more dubious acquisitions and poachings over the years, there was a land-based pecking order, where successive rungs on the property ladder looked up or down, depending on where one was located by the scattershot accident of birth. I had particularly noticed this when I visited my mother's people in the country. They owned a very small parcel of land, typical peasant farmers, but because we, in my family, owned nothing, not even our own house, I was reminded, on a daily basis, not overtly but subtly and unmistakeably that I was at the very bottom of the property pile, which could be only altered by acquiring such accoutrements, and doing so fast, a likelihood that had impossible odds attached to it, as unlikely as Mary Casey up the road, who had some dubious offspring, unconventionally begotten, becoming the Archbishop of Cashel and Emly.

Roisin came home for holidays, and told me all about her experiences at college. I was mad jealous but we had decided that I would stay put until the nightmare was over, whenever that was. I had decided to help my father in the painting trade, a job I had no aptitude or affection for, but one that gave me the opportunity to monitor matters arising in our area. We even worked at the Barracks, painting its vast expanses of walls. The Germans we met were civil enough, but only because we were doing their bidding.

My German was by then good enough to follow conversations and what I was overhearing from them was confirming what Benedict had told us about trouble on the Eastern Front. One day we would see certain personnel, the next day they would be gone. (They reminded me of the Christian Brothers. You never knew who'd be fronting-up the operation on a particular day, so efficient was the top brass, in both bodies, at dispersing errant personnel to far-flung counties, and in some cases, countries.) But it wasn't for reasons of errancy that these men were being shipped out. They were just needed where they could either kill or be killed.

I was able to take a close interest in the building project in the Barracks and the more I appreciated the original scheme, and now as I saw the way in which it was being reconstructed, the more engaged I became in the study of architecture. I resolved that when the Antzies had scuttled away under their stones, that I would study for a degree in that subject. Roisin was well ahead of me, however, but she said she was prepared to allow me to catch up, a commitment that moved me deeply. She said she would go abroad, maybe to Africa and possibly India, to offer her services, until we could marry. (I did point out that I hadn't actually asked her, but we both knew that that was where we were heading.) The welter of imponderables sometimes got me down. I sometimes lost the belief that the centrifugal forces we were caught up in, could ever correct themselves and life get back on to an even keel.

One of my recurring concerns was that the Germans, when they knew the game was up and that the biting east wind sweeping in from Russia, was ending their Reich almost before it had properly begun, would sabotage the Barracks for the second time. For this reason those of us in the FCE who were able to, made it our business to find work in the Barracks and to make sure we were there at the critical hour to ensure the place was left intact when Jerry finally abandoned his doomed ship.

Chapter 17

... all you who are in love...

I was stirring a large container of paint one morning when a German soldier began to take a close interest in what I was doing. I became nervous because the level of suspicion on both sides at that time was at fever-pitch. He offered me a cigarette, which I declined, a refusal which could have been seen as a gesture of hostility. I explained to him in my best German that I didn't smoke, adding, in as friendly a tone as I could muster, that he shouldn't be smoking either. He didn't take offence. He said they received them almost for nothing, and that the same applied to beer and schnapps. He told me that if I wanted either cigarettes or drink he could arrange to supply me with as much of either as I wanted. He seemed over-keen to be friendly. I was doubly suspicious.

I said that it would not be popular in the town if it were known that there was a black market in German fags and booze going on. He said that some of his fellow soldiers were already handing out copious supplies of said items to other workers at the Barracks. This alarmed me as we had decided in our groups that wheeling or dealing with the forces of occupation, whatever the activity, was not to be encouraged.

He asked me a few mornings later if he could speak with me. "My name is Johannes Jung", he told me. I was getting worried at this stage as I was wary that he might be on to me.

'What's your name?' he asked, in that abrupt German way that comes across to us as aggressive.

'Thomas', I replied.

'Can I ask you a private question, Thomas?'

'I'm very busy', I said, trying to fob him off.

'But I won't delay you', he persisted. 'Please vill you come viss me, Thomas? I need badly to talk viss someone from ze town.' There was a shrill insistence in his voice, an urgency which could have been a major trap. This is the last thing I wanted or needed. I decided to give him the benefit of the doubt. We went behind the water tower, out of earshot.

'To talk about what?'

He was in a state of great anxiety.

'I have fallen in love with one of your young women', he said. 'I knew the first time I saw her that she was the woman for me. She is so beautiful, and Irish, and lovely'.

'OK', I said, still wary. 'I get the picture. What do you want me to do about it?'

'Well', he continued, 'can I tell you a secret?'

'Depends on what it is, I suppose', I said.

'I believe the war is lost', he said. This didn't seem to connect with the lead-up.

'By whom?' I cut in.

'By Hitler', he said, 'and between ourselves, I'm very glad. If I were overheard telling you this, I would be marched out and shot against this wall', he said, pointing to the high wall of the water tower. 'And I am not alone in holding ziss opinion. Many of my comrades in this garrison hate everything about Hitler and fascism. I was born in Augsburg, in Bavaria and brought up a Catholic. I was dragooned into the Hitler Youth as a boy. It was the done thing. There was no choice. We had a great time going camping and building bridges and learning about outdoor life. We sat around the campfire at night singing patriotic songs. I thought it was great. But things began to get ugly in the late 1930s when my Jewish friends began first to be insulted openly, then to be seated at the back of the class, then to fail to turn up for school altogether. When I asked where they had gone, I was told to mind my own business. I said it was my business to enquire after my friends. I was told that I shouldn't have Jewish friends, which I found shocking. I used to listen to the BBC and was alarmed at what I was hearing. One evening I was listening to the news – the radio was kept upstairs – and I heard of Kristallnacht. I ran downstairs shouting, to tell my parents about what I had heard. A neighbour had come in to visit us, and when he heard what I blurted out, but more importantly, where I had heard it from, he made a hurried apology and left. He never came into our house again. Whenever we saw him in the street, he pretended he hadn't seen us and looked away. That's how things were, Thomas. Nobody trusted anybody. And that's how it is here in this very Barracks. Some of us Swabians who knew each other since schooldays talk to each other and are fearful for the future. Now I've gone and fallen in love with an Irish girl. To tell you the truth, I've also fallen in love with Ireland, Thomas. I want to stay here and to marry Margaret. There are quite a few of us who feel the same way about your lovely country. We dread the thought of going back to a defeated Germany. It will be a terrible place to live. The things we Nazis have done will haunt us forever. Is there any way you could help me and my friends to stay here after the war is over, provided we are not drafted away to the Russian front in the meantime?'

By this time Johannes was crying. Tears were spilling down his cheeks. This was no act. This young man was totally serious and sincere.

He went on: 'I'm very sorry about the cigarettes and the drink the other day. That was only an awkward way of getting to talk with you. I have been observing you and your father, that kind gentleman you work with. He is your father? No? When I got to know what sort of person you were, I felt safe telling you about my problem with Margaret. I don't know how I will cope if I lose that wonderful girl. You must help me, Thomas. Please help me.' He was pleading with me.

'I'm not sure what I can do', I said. 'How well do you know her?' 'Well enough to know that if I can't be with her, my life has no meaning. My big fear is what should I do if I am sent to the Russian Front? I'm going to refuse to go. I intend to desert. Would the people of this town hide me if I 'went missing'? I'm afraid to put this pressure on Margaret's family, or the people of the town, because my superiors can get very ugly if orders aren't obeyed. We have been on our best behaviour since coming to your town. We love it here. By 'we' I mean my comrades because we are not being asked to do the inhuman things German soldiers are forced to do in other places. And the Tipperary people are so nice to us. We can't believe our luck to have been posted here. The British were so stupid to get on the wrong side of the Irish, who are such a tolerant and patient people.'

'I'll make enquiries, and see what people say, Johannes', I said. 'But don't expect miracles. You say the Irish are so understanding. Yes, we are. But we are also weary of violence. We have come through a ghastly time only 20 years ago and this town is still split down the middle as a result of the messy end of British rule here. The irony is that you people have united us, and healed us, in a way we never would have thought possible. What I'd like to ask you is 'How many in the Barracks agree with your opinions?'

'Not very many, to tell the truth. We have animals here that are busting a gut to cut loose on the Irish people.

They are trained killers. Some of the SS have worked in the concentration camps and have lost their souls. My stomach heaves to listen to their ravings about being the Herrenvolk, the Master Race. They think that, being Aryans, they are at the top of the evolutionary tree, all other races being inferior. Just to look at them and to listen to them is to know that they are the scrapings of the gene pool, dangerous people. They even have that haunted, shaven-headed, soul-less, dangerous look about them. Rather than being at the top, I think they are at the very bottom of the evolutionary tree. Their weak, mostly uneducated, minds have been filled with false notions by the Nazi mind-benders. One sure way of making people feel on top of the world is to tell them falsehoods like being the One-and-Only. Theories of racial superiority are the greatest evil in the whole world, in my view. Even my own Church, the Catholic Church, with its doctrine of being the One, Holy, Catholic, and Apostolic Church is wrong to be claiming to be the only path to salvation, and filling believers' minds with bogus notions of spiritual superiority, that there's no salvation outside the Church. I don't want to be misunderstood here in saying what I'm about to say, and don't draw any unintended conclusions, but the Jewish idea of being the Chosen People is in my opinion equally bonkers – as is the crazy notion that the Promised Land was promised to them by God. None of which, I must most strongly emphasise, justifies the ill-treatment they have and are receiving. But I believe that daft theories like that will just fade away in the future, when people aren't afraid to ask questions.We were taught that our Protestant neighbours would go straight to Hell because they were inferior in faith to us. That can't be right. I stay in the Church because I don't have the courage to go it alone. I should be ashamed of myself. Religion can be a very divisive thing, like politics and racial theories. When this bloody war is over, I never want to hear of any of these wicked lies again. I've had my fill of propaganda. The Bible has a lot to answer for. There is much blood on its pages. Why does humanity have such a strong need for scapegoats? Where I come from, we were full of hope that Adolf Hitler, being Catholic, and having a special relationship with the Vatican, would be a good person to lead Germany. How wrong can one be? And I must also admit to having an ulterior motive for going to mass here each Sunday. It's a guaranteed way of sitting in a place where I can see Margaret for a whole, uninterrupted hour. I have no religious interest in mass but watching Margaret is pure heaven. She and I have special places to sit, and we go early so that we can be sure to be close together. One smile from her sees me through the whole week until I can see her again. Thomas, I appeal to you to help me. Please help me.' The man was distraught.

Chapter 18

… Tipp'rary is as fine a town …

The times we were living through injected a palpable sense of what in Irish was known as tir-ghra – love of country or, more specifically, love of place. It was a much deeper, purer, and maturer emotion than exclusivist, blinkered nationalism. It was even more refined than patriotism, which also had connotations of unhealthy passions, two terms which in Ireland's case were forever sullied by a knee-jerk anti-Englishness, combined with a willingness to shed blood. Tir-ghra was a more deeply and more securely-rooted love. It transcended the warped and thwarted vocabularies of the hate-brigades. One could experience a sense of tir-ghra without denying people of other places their entitlement to have similar feelings about their locales, without anyone being denied their entitlement to a healthy rootedness in one's own cherished place, or feeling that one's own sentiments were somehow caricatures. The mutuality of tir-ghra acted to bond sincere people rather than putting a wedge between them. One didn't have to be long in the company of a typical exponent of a particular strain of Irish nationalism before the 'slagging' or the disparagings began. It usually took the form of an outpouring of distorted anti-English stock phrases that revealed more about the biased speaker than about those who the speaker was besmirching. There was never an opportunity lost to get the little 'dig' in whenever possible. A readiness to take away from what was being said, to take down a peg, to diminish, became almost a conditioned reflex. It served as a conversation-stopper, moving the topic on to safe ground for the speaker. This habit, which passed for humour, was enervating, but it served to remind the company which side the speaker was on. And there were only two sides that mattered, us and the English, and we were goodies, and they were the baddies. This is largely what passed for the culture of nationalism in Ireland, a tedious drip-feed of anti-Britishness. Any mention of royalty, or of the aristocracy, or the privileged classes triggered a diatribe, some tedious put-down or other, before the speaker had even begun. It kept people in a permanent mentality of negativity. Even when such people were being positive, it was a mere detour before getting back to the main business of Brit-bashing. I heard a man one day who happened to speak about being in the company of ex-British officers. Another member of the group, unbidden, said: 'If I was there I'd have shot the f***ers'. When people harbour such knee-jerk enmity, it surely diminishes them. I call it 'the minus-mind'. In such a milieu, the cynic is king.

Now all of that had changed. Now, by a seismic twist of fate, we were on the same side. Now all the learned reflexes were suddenly redundant. But was that conditioned hostility-response now transferred to the Germans? Well, not very obviously. For one, they hadn't been there long enough for enough resentment to build up. For a casual relationship of obloquy to obtain, as people were discovering, there must, ironically, exist a certain quality of love/respect, interspersed with the hate – which did not apply as far as the Germans were concerned, but, and this was a revelation, did exist in relation to the English, for all their faults. Also, the Antzies hadn't committed any known atrocities to put them in the firing-line of people's animosities – not yet. But everyone knew that that day was fast approaching.

People could feel that surge of tir-ghra, particularly in the pubs. There were now more women independently to be seen in pubs, a grand improvement. And they were not segregated in the 'snug' as in olden times, or latched onto a man, but in the open bars, participating in conversation, having their input into the many matters arising daily in the bizarre times the town was living through. A quiet revolution was happening.

It was obvious from the songs and recitations being aired that there things stirring in the deep core of the people. I would, on the odd night, accompany my father to his watering-hole, Jody Kavanagh's. He would treat me to a half-pint, or a 'medium' of Guinness as it was called, served-up in a shapely, fluted glass. My father was asked on occasion for a contribution and he would, always reluctantly, oblige.

One evening he recited a poem he had written himself, entitled Tipp'rary Fair.

TIPP'RARY FAIR

Through childish eyes, those scenes so wild, the beasts corralled in coop and pen,
I beheld with awe, anxious eye and jaw, as cud was chewed and chewed again,
The pavement spattered, schoolchildren scattered, as pungent floes the streets coursed down,
Steps nimbly chosen through beasts by the thousand, at the seasonal fair in Tipp'rary Town.

By early morning, the herds arriving met streets deserted, shops boarded-up;
Plate glass protected, traffic redirected, as drovers parched sought bite and sup.
The bovine denizens took up their residence; with CJ Kickham surveying the scene.
By eight were Main Street, Churchwell and Bridge Street a-heave with haunches, likewise Fair Green.

They grinned tooth-gapped, as hand was slapped and deal was struck and luck returned,

Then outstretched palm creased notes embalmed, while gawking face with interest burned.
Farm hands were hired, the halt retired - their destinies crudely bartered there;
As the farming people, 'neath St Michael's steeple, amassed largesse at Tipp'rary Fair.

But the Christmas Fair, 'mid twinkling glare, was favourite by far for me;
The lamp-lit morning the gloom adorning, shops stacked with toys, a joy to see;
Then streets were purged, last bargains urged, as pub hubbub with song did rise;
Then home unsteady, swayed farmer heady.
Thus marked another year's demise.

He pronounced the town's name as Tipp'rary – three syllables, rather than Tipperary, four syllables. This is because that is how it is pronounced by the people, who rarely use the four syllables. The poem recalls the scenes on the streets of the town and many other towns in Ireland at the quarterly fairs, when towns are taken over by farmers, animals, drovers, dealers and musicians. We had to be careful to wear our wellington boots on those days on our way to school, to wade through the streets greasy from the country-smells of the lavas of slurry, carrying our best shoes in our satchels, and being ultra-careful not to slip.

He had recited this poem in the past, but now it had an added poignancy, for the locations mentioned were held in a place of special affection in people's hearts. The poem brought back sweet memories of the town in other days and was received with appreciative applause.

Then it was Billy Burke's turn to take centre-stage. He obliged, by singing Churchwell Waters:

Tipp'rary is as fine a town
As there is in this nation
O it's well spacious, decked all round
With grove and fine plantation
In Springhouse Grove where young men rove
To court the sweetheart whom we love
That Mallow Spa was ne'er so bright
As our own blessed Churchwell Waters

There is four markets in the year
Our town to adorn
And dealers do come far and near
To do business at the thriving fairs there
You'll find slips and sows, and new milk cows
Sheep and ferrets to be sold
And a handsome girl, I'll be bound
In Tipp'rary you will find her.

There is a bridge all in our town
And under it lie five arches
'Twas never moved by mountain flood
It dreads neither wind nor storm
In those things you see
All custom free
The boys playing in the ball-alley
And in Jody Kav'nagh's you'll get whiskey free
But you'll pay for it in the morning.....

More enthusiastic plaudits: Churchwell was held in great affection among the old residents of the town, its sloping stones worn shiny from generations of children sliding down them. It was often debated what might be behind the words beginning...'In Springhouse Grove.....', whether this referred to a simple love story, or perhaps they contained a deeper level of allegorical meaning, as many Irish songs did?

Then it was Nora Kennedy's turn. Nora is one of the district's best traditional singers. She sang the local ballad Patrick Sheehan, special to our family, penned by Charles J Kickham, the revered Tipperary writer, whose monument graced a place of prominence in Main Street, opposite the Market Yard.

Patrick Sheehan

My name is Patrick Sheehan,
My years are thirty-four;
Tipp'rary is my native place,
Not far from Galtymore;
I came from honest parents,
But now they're lying low;
And many's the pleasant day I spent
In the Glen of Aherlow.

My father died; I closed his eyes
Outside our cabin door;
The landlord and the sheriff too
Were there the day before!
And then my loving mother
And sisters three also
Were forced to go with broken hearts
From the Glen of Aherlow.

For three long months, in search of work,
I wandered far and near;
I went then to the poor-house,
For to see my mother dear;
The news I heard nigh broke my heart;
But still in all my woe,
I blessed the friends who made their graves
In the Glen of Aherlow.

Bereft of home and kith and kin,
With plenty all around,

I starved within my cabin;
And slept upon the ground;
But cruel as my lot was,
I ne'er did hardship know
Till I joined the British Army
Far away from Aherlow.

'Rouse up, there,' says the Corporal,
'You lazy Irish hound;
Why don't you hear, you sleepy dog,
The call 'To Arms' sound?'
Alas I had been dreaming
Of days long, long ago;
I woke before Sebastapol,
And not in Aherlow.

I groped to find my musket -
How dark I thought the night!
O Blessed God, it was not dark,
It was the broad daylight!
And when I found that I was blind,
My tears began to flow;
I longed for even a pauper's grave
In the Glen of Aherlow.O Blessed Virgin Mary,
Mine is a mournful state;
A poor blind prisoner here I am,
In Dublin's dreary gaol;
Struck blind within the trenches,
Where I never feared the foe;
And now I'll never see again
My own sweet Aherlow.

A poor neglected mendicant,
I wander through the street;
My nine months pension now being out,
I beg from all I meet:
As I joined my country's tyrants,
My face I'll never show
Among the kind old neighbours
In the Glen of Aherlow.

Now Irish youths, dear countrymen,
Take heed of what I say;
If you join the English regiments,
You'll surely rue the day;
And whenever you are tempted
A soldiering to go,
Remember poor blind Sheehan
From the Glen of Aherlow.

The work-house mentioned on the song was now part of the Barracks complex, draped in forbidding red Swastikas, a fact which would have registered with the clientele of the public house. There were such ugly drapings on many other buildings in the town, something that was intolerable to the locals, but which we chose to live with, until such time as the world came to its senses and erased the trauma of the present.

Nora's eye caught my father's for 'twas well-known that we were the selfsame Sheehans as the Patrick in the song. The cherished Glen was deeply etched into the inner topography of the Tipperary people, and when Nora sang: '..... And many's the pleasant day I spent, In the Glen of Aherlow', everyone present nodded in silent assent, for the Glen had that effect on all who were inspired by its sweeping splendour, our local version of paradise, crowned by the gracious grandeur of Galteemore.

The musicians present, on fiddle, whistle, uileann pipes, and bodhran, kept the ball rolling between songs with Bonny Kate, St Ann's Reel, the Copperplate, O'Carolan's Concerto, Polkas, Hornpipes, Set Dances...

Jody Kavanagh's voice could be heard rising above the tumult with his favourite, the Galbally Farmer:

The Galbally Farmer

One evening of late as I happened to stray,
To the county Tipp'rary I straight took my way,
To dig the potatoes and work by the day,
I hired with a Galbally farmer.
I asked him how far we were bound for to go.
The night it was dark, and the north wind did blow.
I was hungry and tired and my spirits were low,
For I got neither whiskey nor cordial.

This miserable miser he mounted his steed
To the Galbally mountains he posted with speed;
And surely I thought that my poor heart would bleed
To be trudging behind that old naygur.
When we came to his cottage I entered it first;
It seemed like a kennel or ruined old church:
Says I to myself, "I am left in the lurch
In the clutches of Darby O'Leary."

I well recollect it was Michaelmas night,
To a hearty good supper he did me invite,
A cup of sour milk that would physic a snipe—
'Twould give you the trotting disorder.
The mouldy potatoes would poison the cats,
The barn where my bed was was swarming with rats,
'Tis little I thought it would e'er be my lot
To lie in that hole until morning.

By what he had said to me I understood,
My bed in the barn it was not very good;
The blanket was made at the time of the flood;
The quilt and the sheets in proportion.
'Twas on this old miser I looked with a frown,
When the straw was brought out for to make my shake down.
I wished that I'd never seen Galbally town,
Or the sky over Darby O'Leary.

I worked in Kilconnell, I worked in Kilmore,

I worked in Knockainy and Shanballymore,
In Pallas and Nicker and Sollohedmore,
With decent respectable farmers:

I worked in Tipperary, the Rag, and Rosegreen,
At the moat of Kilfeakle, the Bridge of Aleen,
But such woeful starvation I never yet seen
As I got from old Darby O'Leary.

And now it is time for to finish my song
I hope that the reign of this breed be soon gone
So here's to that day – for it won't be too long
And bad cess to you Darby O'Leary.

The cries of approbation that greeted the words: 'I hope that the reign of this breed be soon gone', were rapturous. Normally, he sang 'his breed', but the clientele know very well what Jody had in mind.

Not to be outdone, his wife Carmel piped up with the Bansha Peeler:

The Bansha Peeler

The Bansha peeler went out one night,
On duty a-patrolling, O
He met a goat upon the road
Who took him to be a-strolling, O
With bayonets fixed he sallied forth,
And caught him by the wizen, O,
And then swore out a mighty oath
He'd send him off to prison, O.

'O, mercy, sir,' the goat replied;
'Pray, let me tell my story, O.

I am no Rogue or Ribbonman,
No Croppy, Whig or Tory, O.
I am guilty not of any crime
Of petty or high treason, O,
And I'm badly needed at this time,
For this is the ranting season, O.'

Chorus:
Meg a geg geg let go o' me leg
Or I'll puck you with me horn O
Let Bansha be. Let go of me
Or I'll leave you bruised and torn O

Peeler:
'It is in vain for to complain,
Or give your tongue such bridle, O,
You're absent from your dwelling place,
Disorderly and idle, O.
Your hoary locks will not avail,
Nor your sublime oration, O,
For Grattan's Act will you transport,
By your own information, O.

Chorus

Goat:
'This parish and this neighbourhood
Are peaceable and tranquil, O;
There's no disturbance here, Thank God,
And long may it continue so.
I don't regard your oath a pin,
Nor sign for my committal, O,
For my jury will be gentlemen,
To grant me an acquittal, O.

Chorus

Peeler:
'I'll soon chastise your impudence
And violent behaviour, O;
Well bound to Cashel you'll be sent,
Where you will find no favour, O.
The magistrates will all consent
Will sign your condemnation, O,
And from there to Cork you will be sent
For speedy transportation, O.'

Chorus

Goat:
'No Penal Law have I transgressed,
By need or combination, O;
I have no certain place of rest,
No home nor habitation, O.
But Bansha is my dwelling-place,
Where I was bred and born, O,
I'm descended from an honest race,
That's all the trade I've learned, O.'

Chorus

'Let the consequence be what it will,
A peeler's power I'll let you know!
I'll fetter you at all events
And march you off to prison, O.
For sure, you rogue, you can't deny
Before a judge and jury, O,
Intimidation with your horns
And threatening me with fury, O,'

Chorus

'Tis plain to me that you are drunk
On whiskey, rum or brandy, O,

You would not have such gallant spunk,
Or be so bold or manly, O.
You readily would let me pass
If I'd the money handy, O,
To treat you to a poteen glass -O,
'Tis then I'd be the dandy, O!'

Chorus

This old 19th century favourite, which mocked the forces of law and order, was the work of the poet Darby Ryan of Bansha. It expressed with wit and perspicacity the uneasy relationship the Irish have with legal systems that they themselves had no part in creating. And that also went for Church laws.

I had never heard such an outpouring of local balladry. I felt elated to know that there was such thought-provoking talent to be found on my very own doorstep.

'One voice! One voice!' I heard over the din. And then Monica O'Shea could be heard singing the Little Drummer Boy:

The Little Drummer Boy

One fine summer's morning both gallant and gay
A group of young ladies through Tipp did parade
A regiment of soldiers it chanced to pass by
A drummer in one of them he soon cocked his eye.

He went to his comrade and to him did say
'Twenty four ladies I saw yesterday,
One of them ladies she have me heart won
And if she deny me I'm fairly undone.'

'Now go to that lady and tell her your mind
Tell her she has wounded your poor heart inside
Tell her she has wounded you heart very sore

And if she deny you, what can she do more?'

'Twas early next morning the young man arose
He dressed himself up in a fine suit of clothes
A watch in his pocket, a cane in his hand
He saluted the girls as they followed the band.

He came up to her and he said 'Pardon me,
Pardon me lady for making so free
My hon'rable lady you have me heart won
And if you deny me I'm fairly undone'.

'Be off little drummer, now what do you mean?
For I'm the lord's daughter from Ballykisteen
I'm a lord's daughter who's honoured you see
Be off little drummer you're making too free'.

He put on his hat and he bade her farewell
Saying 'I'll send my soul soon to heaven or hell
For with this long pistol that hangs by my side
I'll put an end to an ould dreary life'.

'Come back little drummer now don't take it ill
For I wouldn't like to be guilty of sin
To be guilty of innocent blood for to spill
Come back little drummer I'm here at your will,

And we'll hire a car and to Bansha we'll go
There we'll get married in spite of our foes
What can they say when it's over and done
For I fell in love with the rowl of yer drum'.

Bansha was figuring prominently tonight. With all the mentions of drummers and regiments this song was clearly an import, no doubt brought to Tipp by a British soldier of the old dispensation, but now seamlessly absorbed into the native canon. It demolishes the taboo on inter-marriage both between and castes and the tribes. Love finds a way. It reminded me of Johannes' and Margaret's predicament.

An unmistakable voice arose from the outbreak of chatter that followed Nora's song, the voice of Bobby Fleming, raising the rafters. He loved the song Bohercrowe, about a famous victory by a local team in the 1880s, in the early years of the Gaelic Athletic Association, the much loved GAA .

Bohercrowe

Bohercrowe is the darlin'
Bohercrowe is not bet (beat) yet
Rosanna may be saddled
But yet she need not fret
When the boys met Fethard
Their medals they did get
Good Luck to Bohercrowe
For we are the Champions yet!

Mikey Ryan from time to time
Was noted for his kick
And ev'ry time he got the ball
He put it in the net!
Yes, when the boys met Fethard
Their medals they did get
Good luck to Bohercrowe
For we are the Champions yet!
Coming through Kilfeakle
It was a glorious sight
To see the Hills of Bohercrowe
Ablaze with fires that night
Coming through the Spittal
Without dread nor fret
Good Luck to Bohercrowe

For we are the Champions yet!

Bobby pronounced the place-name Bohercrowe as 'Bore-a-crowe'.

If the historians of Gaelic football are to be trusted and that game took place in the late1880s, the cheers and whoops and hollers that greeted that song were as immediate as the adulations which greeted the team the night they brought the Cup home to the town over 50 years before, as if the Cup, and Mikey Ryan and the members of the victorious team, were present in the pub that very night. One could sense the stirring of deep emotions. It told you something about Tipperary people.

Then we heard the unmistakable voice of Billy Keating, who fancied himself as the local bard. He lived in The Barracks, and had penned a few verses in honour of current developments. He'd had a few pints by this stage of the evening, and his voice was getting slurred. There had been a bit of an argument about poetry a few nights earlier. Billy's adversary, 'getting it up' for Billy, was praising the poetry of people like Yeats, Hopkins, William Blake. Billy was having none of it. 'They're not poets', he said disparagingly, 'I'd poet the shite out of any of 'em'.

He cleared his throat to alert the audience, simultaneously breaking wind, which caused gales of laughter. 'Never mind', said Billy. 'Merely an idle wind that comes from the heart. And ignorant people call it a fart'. More laughter.

Then he began:

Glenview Square

The houses, ranged

Rectangular,
Thirty-six in all, there are;
The 'Back', the ' Front'
Two-up, two-down
Half a mile from Tipp'rary Town.

Past Airmount
And the railway station
The Abbey School, for some education
Past St. Vincent's
For healing and prayer
Down the hill, lies Glenview Square.

Built in Queen Victoria's era
The Barracks stands
As a chimera
To rude ambition...
An Imperial dream,
An ill-starr'd impulse, run out of steam.

Like mountain goats
We shinned the walls
Surveyed the Square, where once the calls
Of sergeant-major
Drilling troops
As locals watched them jump through hoops.

This gifted jewel,
By fanatic few
Was reduced to ashes in '22
They pricked for ever
The imperial bubble
And reduced this gifted jewel to rubble.

Where British Might
Was once on view
The modern age yields purpose new
Instead of Reveille
Last Post blaring
Achtung, Schneller Marsch is now for the hearing.

We faced down the wrath of the Black and Tan
Who tasted the backlash of the Irish man
We'll not let the Hun be master
We won't be ruled by Nazi bastards.

There was a feeling that Billy had overstepped the mark and was in danger of becoming rather too political, and before he could dig an even deeper hole for himself, the landlord intervened. 'Good man yourself, Billy', he said, 'we'll hear the rest of that another night', to general agreement.

When Billy had been diplomatically gagged, a group of German soldiers, who had been drinking up in a far corner of the pub, who fortunately hadn't heard the details of his contribution, getting carried away with the bonhomie and banter, decided unbidden to make their contribution to the evening's session. They burst into the Horst Wessel Song. The atmosphere in the pub froze, people instantly sobering-up. The soldiers weren't a minute into their raucous anthem when they, one-by-one, became aware that they had transgressed and trodden on sacred ground. Drunk as they were, their words turned to dust in their mouths when they realised the enormity of their faux pas. It suddenly dawned on them that they weren't nearly as well-integrated as they thought they were. An embarrassed silence pervaded the premises after the euphoria of the earlier hours . Nothing was said. Nothing was needed. They stood up, awkwardly, self-consciously, made their apologies and left, hoping that their indiscretion would not reach the ears of their superiors.

The atmosphere of that magical night was sabotaged, not intentionally, but sabotaged nevertheless. There were no further offerings.

All those in that pub that night were reminded, if reminder were necessary, that the greatest challenge we had ever faced, even greater than the heroics of the stalwart Tipperary people of the past, presently confronted us, all of us.

There was no one on the fence this time. There was no fence.

The musicians, unbidden, ended the evening with the plaintive air Ar Eireann Ni Neosfhainn Ce Hi, their traditional anthem to end such sessions. Then we bade each other Oiche Mhaith, Good Night, and wended our ways philosophically homewards.

Chapter 19

... old foes meet... the world turned upside down...

'Greetings, Mr de Valera. Please be seated. Sorry I can't offer anything more fitting that these insalubrious premises for our meeting. They don't call it Colditz for nothing. I hope you and your party aren't suffering unduly. I suppose that under the circumstances we should be grateful to be meeting at all. I trust a pot of tea will suffice as a beverage. That suits you more than it suits me, I believe.'

He moved closer. 'I do have the wherewithal to spirit me from off this mortal coil, as I'm sure you do also, but this is not the hour to be contemplating such unpatriotic opt-outs. Are they treating you well?'

'Yes, thank you'.

'We must talk, Sir. In fact it's high time we two talked and got down to brass tacks. To back-track a bit, had we met earlier, had you led the Treaty delegation, and we had talked back then, I believe that much subsequent turmoil might have been avoided. You do appreciate that your inexplicable failure to travel put Mr Collins in an impossible predicament. Or maybe you don't'.

'Am I here to be lectured-to?'

'We need to talk man-to-man, Mr de Valera. I am of the view that this war can't last much longer than a few months, now that the Russians, the Chinese, and the Americans are piling pressure on Hitler. No, Sir, I don't mean to lecture you – far from it. I merely meant that had we two talked in 1921, common sense might have prevailed and you could, more easily, have contained your wilder associates. What you have done now in your momentous change of policy, in breaking the logjam between our peoples, will redound to your credit down the ages. It was my hope during the Treaty Talks to take them as far as they could be taken, as a prelude to completing the job as soon as the dust had settled, and you must agree there were clouds of dust obscuring visibility on both sides. Your presence would have made it possible for the things I wished to say to you in strict privacy, to be said. A great burden was placed on the shoulders of Mr Collins – whom it should be said was considerably younger than either of us, although I have some years on you. Eight I think. He was quite right in his assessment that the Treaty represented the freedom to obtain freedom. Reading between the lines of that statement was the key to the truth of the matter. In poor old Collins's case, both the message and the Messenger got shot. The Six Counties option was not, nor could not be, a permanent answer to the so-called Irish Question. A nine-county Northern Ireland could, demographically, have worked, but not politically. Any fool could have seen that. The ancient ties between our peoples are too interlocking to permit of the simplistic fracture that your purists, perhaps even including yourself, were hell-bent on achieving. But these are speculations for historians at future dates, Mr de Valera. Can I call you Eamon?'

'Yes, Mr Churchill'.

'Winston. Please.'

'Mr Churchill is fine'.

'I seem to be doing all the talking'.

'Isn't that what you are best at?' Dev said, tongue visibly in cheek.

'Come, come, Eamon. We are the democratic leaders of our peoples, holed up in this dungeon, and none too sure we'll get out alive'.

'I've been holed-up in dungeons before'.

'Indeed you were, and I must admit to laughing out loud when I heard how you had out-witted, out-foxed, out-manoeuvred us by escaping from Lincoln Prison. They should make a moving picture of it one day. And I must admit that the reasons you were there were trumped up. You and your fellow freedom-fighters were making us look like idiots. We were smarting at what we saw as treachery on your part by referring to the Hun as your 'gallant allies in Europe'. That felt like a slap in the face with a cold fish to us. We were also painfully aware that had Ireland been granted all that you and your colleagues were demanding, it would have had an unstoppable domino-effect on our much cherished Empire – an Empire that we expected to last somewhat longer than it has. In this regard, you have been more visionary than we have. The Empire is no more. Whatever remains of the, hopefully fraternal, amalgam of nations and territories that comes out of the mincing-machine that this war has proven to be, is anybody's guess. A Commonwealth of sorts, I guess, certainly not an empire.'

'I thought that a Commonwealth meant just that – a sharing of wealth, hence common wealth'.

'We're not communists, no more than you are. That's taking the idea too literally. Wealth comes in all guises. Freedom is wealth of sorts, you of all people must agree with that. And natural beauty, the Lakes of Killarney, the Cliffs of Moher, the Glen of Aherlow, the Grianan of Aileach - isn't that wealth of sorts?'

Dev muttered to himself: 'You can't eat scenery' and more audibly: 'Don't be expecting a united Ireland to be an automatic member of your "Commonwealth"'.

'Why ever not? We shall all be coming to the table as equals now, Eamon, when this dark night for the soul of civilisation is over. We British have been well and truly knocked off our imperial high horse by the collapse of our security forces, by the humiliation of invasion, and having to endure a conquest of sorts. No longer can or should the Scots, the Welsh or the Irish think of us as overlords, and I must admit, our behaviour over the centuries did lead them to think so. Gone is the braggadocio of the past, the strutting, the superiority complex, the bellowing public school accent. We have learned much in the last few years. We are like the vicar who knelt down to pray for humility. "Dear God", he began, "I am beseeching you to make me humble, for you and only know how important I am. That about sums us up Eamon; we're like the Jesuits – tops in humility, or we were. But old habits do die hard, I must admit that.

One thing I have been thinking a lot about here in my eyrie is the way we English have treated Ireland. We must accept our share of responsibility for pushing Ireland too far. If the shoe had been on the other foot, and roles reversed, I must admit, I'd most probably have done as you did. The perfunctory execution of the leaders in '16 was a godawful error, in hindsight. (Between ourselves, I think it wouldn't have taken the Irish people long to realise what oddballs Pearse and Connolly actually were, had they been released without fanfare after a cooling-down period, their thunder would have been stolen. Pearse was on the verge of bankruptcy. That school of his, a brain-washing centre, more like, was not offering what could be described as a liberal education. MacNeill saw that. . When I read that Pearse was of the opinion that Ireland's population could grow to 20 million or thereabouts, I wondered what planet the man lived on. He was a mystic, a dreamer. As for the brilliant Connolly, he never overcame the rage he internalised as a young man and as a soldier.) I also personally deeply regret sending over the Black and Tans. That merely served to irresponsibly pour petrol on the flames. With the War ending, we had so many imponderables on our plate I'm afraid Ireland got short shrift. In the heat of the moment, colossal errors of judgement were made, each of us on our side trying to out-trump the other in defending what we saw as John Bull's best interests, and to hell with the casualties. Take Amritsar. What a shameful blot on our escutcheon. And all the other shameful episodes, the famines we should have done more to alleviate, and not just in Ireland, in India also, a shocking recent famine, millions dead. We treated Casement, a high-minded man, abominably. So what if he was homosexual. It wasn't anything that those of us who had attended Public Schools were unfamiliar with. I myself had summed up the Navy as; rum, sodomy and the lash. We were way out of our depth in trying to run the Empire. I shall be personally apologising to the Irish people for the mishandling of Irish affairs by London, going back centuries. Religion and politics are a bad mix, Eamon. The Plantations were inexcusable, as were the Scottish Clearances. We looked upon the Welsh as if they were troglodytes. And there are many people in England who have still not excused the Enclosure Acts of the 18th century. The injustices done to so many are neatly summed up by this rhyme:

The law looks harsh on man or woman
Who steals the goose from off the common
But what can be that man's excuse
Who steals the common from the goose?

We behaved like medieval despots. With regard to the Irish Famine, our mean-spirited performance, ostensibly in the name of adhering to economic doctrine, whatever that is, was criminal. The Irish people, reduced to destitution by the whims of cruel fate, needed a tidal wave of generosity from us that never was forthcoming. All they got was a dribble. We, in good faith, had set up Poorhouses, like the one in Tipperary in the early 1840s, which in normal circumstances might have proved adequate. But the Famine, happening at a time of rapidly rising population, ripped such provisions from their moorings, a flimsy umbrella in a hurricane. It was said that the Famine was an Act of God. Now I hear you are a religious man, Eamon, but if that's God for you, count me out. That unfeeling God is no use to me. I was asked by a selection panel once what my religious beliefs were. I could see it was a trip-wire laid to set me up for a tumble. 'Would you consider yourself a pillar of the Church, Mr Churchill?', a po-faced old bigot asked me. I had to think fast on my seat. I was trapped. The Injuns were circling the wagons.

'Well, hardly a pillar', I answered as nonchalantly as possible. 'My support for that estimable institution would be more from the outside. Rather than a pillar, supporting from the inside, think of me more like a flying buttress'. A chuckle went round the table, but not from him. But I did get the nomination. (To be totally honest, I borrowed the metaphor from GM Trevelyan.)'

A thin, suppressed smile broke on de Valera's lips.

'I have been giving serious thought to what comes next, Eamon, when all this pandemonium is over and we are back home. If I am spared, I shall be proposing the dissolution of the old Union as we have known it. It outlived its usefulness long ago. The subterfuge that went on at the passing of the Act of Union with Scotland was shady to say the least. Burns wasn't far out, back then, with his 'parcel of rogues' ballad. And the Irish Act of Union was a travesty, and possibly unconstitutional, such was the arm-twisting and chicanery that were needed to get it through. We of course were terrified of what was going on in France, at the time, and feared its spread, hence the savage putting-down of the 1798 Rebellion. But the nobility of Ireland's stance over the years has convinced me of the need for a completely new beginning. I am going to propose a Tariff Free Zone between what we call the 'Home Nations' of Ireland, Scotland, Wales and England. I remember back in 1896 as a young officer in Bangalore, I heard an Irish soldier singing an old Napoleonic ballad called the Bonny Bunch of Roses. It contained the lines: 'And England, Ireland, Scotland', - (the Bonny Bunch of Roses in the ballad) - 'their unity shall ne'er be broke' – you may know it. It left a deep impression on me, Eamon. When you and your fellow revolutionaries made your brave stand in 1916, it grieved me to the marrow. For all the mistakes, all the preening popinjay shows of arrogance which we English have got up to, down the years there is a genuine, deep affection there for Ireland and for the Irish people. If I could be personal here – there is, I believe, more affection for the Irish among the English than there is for either the Welsh or the Scots, even combined. That, I believe is the truth. We have gone quiet about Ireland in the last twenty years. Why? Not because we have nothing to say, not by a long chalk. Partly shame; partly embarrassment; partly anger! The time has come for a conversation of equals. We were conquered by the Romans. You weren't. Come to think of it, a good dose of Roman discipline did us Celtic Brits no harm. You had an influx of grizzled old reactionary Druids abandoning Celtic Britain and washing up in Ireland in those times, who left their inflexible mark on Irish society, and not necessarily for the good. Patrick bravely took them on. You have, indeed, had your own fill of a different kind of Romish influence since those days, not always a happy stamp, either, I've noticed. I appreciate I am on thin ice here. But, all things considered, I've often thought that if we could combine the best qualities of the Irish with the best of the English, we'd have a pretty good mix. I think that left to their own devices, the Irish, being a more egalitarian people, would have embraced the Reformation ideas more readily than the English, who are naturally a more hierarchical, conservative, and believe it or not, Catholic lot.

I believe that the freedom to travel freely between our islands will be enshrined in our New Confederation. Legislation will be passed to end the nonsense of a

Protestant monarchy, maybe justifiable in its day, but way out of line in modern times. O'Connell could see that. That'll put Orange noses out of joint. Some of those bigots, who are too ready to hurl insults like Anti-Christ at all those who don't fit in with their narrow prejudices, will receive a rude awakening. For too long they have been treated as a museum-piece, a protected species in the zoo of antiquated fossils. Well the zoo is about to be closed down, Eamon. Primogeniture surely also has to go. That other bastion of privilege, the House of Lords is in for the chop. It greatly complicated things with the Home Rule Bill, a shameful example of toffs protecting their own. You haven't forgotten I used to be a Liberal in a previous political incarnation? If any constituent party to the new Confederation wants autonomy on matters like defence or foreign policy, they shall have it. I'd like the bonds that hold us together to be both longer, but stronger. If Ireland wishes to call itself a Republic, and have its own Head of State, then so be it. I love our Union, but I'm afraid I strive in vain to generate much love for many dour unionists, particularly the type Northern Ireland breeds. What was it the poet Maurice James Craig said?:

"It's to hell with the future we'll live in the past

May the Lord in his mercy be kind to Belfast".

The year 1690 is etched into their psyches. Well, it is time for it to be un-etched.

And speaking of Belfast and other locations north of the Border, the need for that absurd so-called Marching Season will wither on the vine. The original reason for it was to keep the Catholic population in its place. Any attempt to say otherwise is either devious or disingenuous. It is my hope that the excessive numbers of marches that people have to tolerate will drop like a stone. The era of Croppies Lie Down is well and truly over. It is also my view that objections to unwelcome marches will not only come from disgruntled Catholics. Many Protestant residents are sick and tired of these quasi-military posturings. The Orange Order is a relic of an embarrassing past, Eamon, and the only reason they try it on is that they know they have had the backing of British might. But not any longer. Yes the army and police could always be relied on to wade in if necessary, but the generality of the British people have no truck with what 17th century ravings the Orange Order believes in, whatever they are. For the life of me I don't know. What I do know is that it stinks. With the end of the Protestant Ascendancy, its raison d'etre will have been swept aside. 'Twas always said of the Ulster unionist that he was more interested in the half-crown than the actual Crown. Had southern Ireland been a runaway economic success-story, they most probably would have had a different take on things. It goes without saying that the pendulum will not be allowed to swing to the other pole and nationalistic marches become a menace in areas where they are not welcome. But that will be an issue for the All-Ireland parliament. The Croppies may no longer be lying down, but for them to become the new repressive ascendancy would be a grave step backwards.

It is my fervent hope that as a result of the wave of goodwill that will flow in Ireland's direction following these seismic times, that the raw anti-English form of Irish nationalism that has taken root and marinated in the last twenty-odd years will be softened and the relationship we forge will phase out the crude separatism of the past. For you must agree Eamon that the extreme, absolute, break-the-connection-with-England rantings you and your colleagues were fighting for would have been in nobody's interest in the long run. We are interdependent peoples, in the heel of the hunt. What is of overarching importance to me is that the Bonny Bunch of Roses remains intact, that the ties that bind us as peoples are sacrosanct, that they are deepened and strengthened, especially in the days that are ahead. We have far more in common with each other than any one of us has with either Europe or America, or them with us. Time will prove this to be true. Britain is broke. We are all broke. I believe the Germans have undertaken elaborate schemes in your country, like the rebuilding of the Tipperary Barracks, of all things, the torching of which struck us at the time as an act of excessive vandalism. And I hear they have plans to re-roof Tintern Abbey and Rievaulx – employing slave labour! They must see themselves as re-incarnated Romans or Normans, dazzling the people with spectacular buildings. As I said earlier Eamon had we not been so pig-headed back in Parnell's time, much aggravation could have been avoided. The Reforms I am proposing will, I believe find common cause with all sectors of political opinion in Britain, whatever the outcome of the next election. If anything, Labour will be keener than my lot, a caste always ready to fight progress. The people will go for the Beveridge proposals in a future election, if we ever escape this trial.

But whoever picks up the torch of governance after this calamity, I shall be arguing for a defence agreement among free nations. What we have just witnessed should serve to demonstrate to the Irish people that fence-sitting is not a viable option in the future. I shall also be pushing the idea of closer economic ties between European nations, to lock us all in together. So-called civilised Europe can never again be allowed to pull down the pillars of an ordered world, to plunge humanity into chaos. But I shall be reserving a place of special affection for the family of the Bonny Bunch of Roses.

Mr Taoiseach, thank you for the statesmanship you and your government have demonstrated in confronting this monster, Hitler. If he comes out alive from this Holocaust, he and his crew will be tried for war crimes, but not only for war crimes, - for breach-of-the-peace crimes, for grave crimes and for petty crimes, for crimes against democracy, for crimes against the helpless, the defenceless and the handicapped, for crimes against humanity. Capital punishment would be too kind for him. We shall have to be vigilant for there will be a scurrying of rats scuttling off the sinking ship. We have our people on the lookout for them. I trust you will provide personnel also. You have missionaries in South America to which he and his fellow scurriers will try to escape'.

There was a period of silence between the two erstwhile enemies.

Eventually Dev spoke.

'Thank you, Winston'.

He seemed to be speaking from a very far-away place, in an abstracted tone of voice.

'Relations between our peoples have indeed been poisoned, mostly though not exclusively, by English intransigence. And of course there were some home-grown obstinates, people like our illustrious Dubliner Mr 'Moses' Carson himself, who led the Unionists into the wilderness and convinced them that they were a Chosen People in a Promised Land of sorts – but promised by whom? Promised by a Stuart dynasty who owned nothing, who had no authority, no right to give or promise anything, who treated people who had lived on lands for centuries as squatters. We know only too well where such delusional thinking leads people. I must agree we produced some inflexibles on our side too, down the years. The depredation of our country, which was treated as a dummy-run for the conquests to come, much like the unclaimed expanses of America, Australia, and wherever the white-man landed, has left deep scars, and some recompense will be sought. The shadow of Cromwell hasn't disappeared. The same goes for India, to name but one other country that was plundered by your imperialists. What would such a sum look like? The true extent of such a figure would not be reckonable, and anything that could be payable, particularly in these straitened times, would be an insult. There are fortunes still being enjoyed that were amassed on the backs of slaves, and other exploited groups, fortunes creamed-off from sugar, cotton, diamonds, tobacco. How can such wrongs be expiated? Anyway, this is not the time to talk of such matters, but mark my words it is an issue that will re-surface, again and again. There are still those who own vast acreages simply because their forbears were the henchmen of William the Conqueror, or Henry VIII, posers sitting on monastic lands. And you can talk of a Commonwealth? How radical do you or a Labour government if it is elected, propose to be, that's what I'd like to know, an answer I await with interest?

I also have had time for reflection, Winston, and I must say, here and now, that my decision, and it was largely my decision, to plunge Ireland into Civil War is the greatest regret of my life. I now realise it went against everything I hold dear. For one, it wasn't a Just War. For a war to be considered Just there must be some likelihood of success. I led my people up a blind alley. There was no chance of us anti-Treatyites changing anything – not the British angle on things, nor the intransigence of the Unionists. Secondly, it was an affront to democracy. It was largely cussedness and vengeance that impelled us. I am glad to have said this, finally. I shall also say it to the Irish people. We have marinated in our own bitter juices for too long.

One of the happiest outcomes of the debate following the end of our neutrality policy, and which I personally welcome, has been the flowering of aspects of the Irish psyche that were previously suppressed or just dormant. I also welcome the things you are saying concerning a new beginning, a level post-war playing field, and when I say this I'm sure I am speaking for the Irish people - '

Churchill cut in: 'Well you have an advantage over me there Eamon', he said, with a wry smirk on his face. 'You once famously said that if you wanted to know what the Irish people wished for, you only have to look into your own heart. When I want to know what the English want, my heart is the last place I'd search. All I'd find there is a baying cacophony'.

de Valera shot him a withering look before continuing. He was not amused.

'We shall redraft our Constitution when the outline of the new Confederation takes shape, enshrining those freedoms that are taken for granted in more liberal societies, and the abuse of which have been highlighted by recent rude awakenings, to put it politely. The Catholic Church wields far too much power in my country, a situation that must be tackled as soon as the war is behind us. The situation that was allowed to get out of hand post-Famine must now be reined-in. The Church became a mini-State, a state within a state. The Bishops dictated policy, making politicians look like messenger-boys. So, between the Church, and the rump of the IRA both claiming to be the spiritual/political guardians of the nation, both claiming to be the legitimate (albeit unelected) government of the country no less – by some sort of apostolic hand-me-down, a mad claim if ever there was one... in all these clashing claims and counter-claims, the people don't know who is in charge. For a Church to control over 90% of the schools in any state is medieval. There will be an end to craven obeisance to those whose first allegiance is not to our state but to a foreign potentate. We don't even know who employs our teachers, the church or the state. You in England confronted this anomaly 400 years ago. Now we must do the same. The tragedy for Ireland is that in those 400 years the people have been prevented from accessing a religion-free liberal education – thanks to your lot, bizarrely for outlawing Catholicism. I too have had many hours in which to ponder the cul-de-sacs we have found ourselves trapped-in. Now is the time for great leaps forward all round.

The Ulster Unionists did, at the time, have objections to coming in with the South, some good, many unworthy. These anomalies will all be removed, leaving the way clear for all but the most blinkered to flourish in a modern Ireland. They said we were backward and underdeveloped economically. Those objections will no longer apply. They said we were priest-ridden, that Home Rule would be Rome Rule. Not anymore. The very same freedoms that you enshrine in Britain will be all available in Ireland. And more, it'll be a nicer place to live. You may even consider retiring to Ireland yourself.

I trust you will recognise from our words and actions how resolved we are that Hitler should be stopped. We Irish I'm afraid can have a circuitous way of failing to getting round to what needs to be said on difficult matters. Well, not any more. When it comes to denouncing the Brits, or the Unionists, we were never short of the bitter word – dehumanisation is a two-way street. But for too long we were guilty of being circumspect on a much greater evil: that of fascism. We are happy to have finally cut through all those thickets. And speaking of anomalies, for how much longer will your Head of State, be also Head of the Church?'

'I couldn't agree more. Our worlds have and will be turned upside down. It is a privilege having Ireland on board in putting it to rights. We shall meet again, Mr de Valera, when the hurly-burly is done.'

'We shall, Mr Churchill. Please convey my warmest personal best wishes, and those of the Irish people to your Royal Family who I believe are also confined in this forbidding place, to your own family, to your government, and to your people.'

'Thank you, Sir, I shall and likewise to your government, to your own wife and family and to the Irish people'.

The meeting ended with a warm handshake.

Chapter 20

… skeletons in cupboards …

Things were moving rapidly in the Eastern theatre of war. Having convinced himself that he had achieved compliance in the western states of Europe, Hitler sucked back the bulk of the non-essential manpower which he had flooded into the seaboard nations of Europe and assembled them in an army of alarming potency, and trundled eastwards.

The transportation of so many humans, with all the logistical challenges that that entails might be a grandiose dream in the fetid imagination of a megalomaniac but the hour-by-hour hazards encountered crossing Poland and Belarus proved tortuous, insurmountable.

One of the first actions taken by the Russians was to decommission every railway line within 50 miles of Moscow. It was going to be 100, but by opting for 50, the Germans were drawn in deeper. Forced marches became obligatory. What became obvious to the German leadership, too late as it transpired, was that the massed forces of Russia, America, and China had taken up 20-mile strategic positions which rendered Moscow impregnable.

In our FCE get-togethers we devoured the ongoing snippets of news that were getting through. Lord Haw Haw was not Hee Heeing so much nowadays. By this time Johannes was daring to attend the odd meeting, a risk that would result in instant execution if he were to be betrayed. He was there the night we were discussing the strange doctrine of Lebensraum. He told us that they had regular lectures on such matters and indeed on every aspect of the thinking behind the Third Reich. He told us that the man who had originally coined the term was Freidrich Ratzel who died in 1904. Ratzel was a geographer and all-round polymath. He developed this theory that all living things need living space – Lebensraum. According to this theory, the people, the Volk, elbow-out other Volk to create living space so that they themselves might flourish. To consolidate their control, they colonise the new territory placing new tenants, of their choosing, on the occupied land.

'This has a strangely déjà vu-ish ring to it', said Mary one of our regular attendees.

'Yes', said Johannes, 'you've a long history of being elbowed-out in your own country. But don't delude yourselves that you are unique. It's an international phenomenon. Believe me. Ratzel said that in order to remain healthy, species must constantly expand the amount of space they occupy. If in the process of occupation you can conveniently classify the indigenous inhabitants in a given land-area as soul-less subhuman aboriginals, it makes the job of clearing the land not much more than a matter of detached efficiency and less messy. Gone is the awkward moral dilemma of slaughtering millions of valuable people, because you can convince yourself that all you are doing is merely cleansing the gene pool. You are merely helping nature get rid of the equivalent of human weeds – pruning the gene-pool in order to create a Master Race. And what could be wrong with that? Future generations, according to this sick theory, will thank us for doing a cleansing job on branches of the human tree that shouldn't have flourished in the first place. It also removes the conscience element of the cleansing process because it allows us to be detached. Press the button, tilt the chute.' It reminded me of the cowboy comics we so enjoyed, in which the Indians, the natives, were called 'pesky varmints' – pestilential vermin.

'Jesus', said Molly, 'that's pure bloody evil. I think I'm going to be sick'.

'Millions have already died in pursuit of Lebensraum', Johannes said. 'Hitler regards the Slavs as subhuman, as well as the Jews and a long list of others. He sees Communism as a Jewish conspiracy. The theory goes that Bolshevism was masterminded by the Jews. Marx was Jewish, Trotsky was Jewish, Lenin was partly Jewish......the list goes disgustingly on.

We were told of a book called The Protocols of the Elders of Zion in one of those talks. It purports to detail the conspiracy in which the Jews take over the world. Can you believe it – global domination no less! As we were being told all this, the thought crossed my mind: If it is OK for Hitler to take over the world, what's wrong with anyone else taking it over? The Communists want global domination as well. Why not the Jews? I of course didn't dare question the lecturer and say that surely the central fallacy of this sort of thinking is the very notion of global conquest in the first place? All imperialisms – whether they be political, religious, ideological, are equally repugnant to me, and I believe should be to all right-thinking people. Go back as far as records go. What is the Old Testament, but a history of empire-building? The original name of The Protocols was 'The Jewish Programme to Conquer the World'. It's a load of plagiarised rubbish. But if it is fed into a preconditioned, ill-informed mind, it will take root and the consequences can be uncontainable. The name of a local priest came up in that talk, a Fr Fahey. He apparently has studied the Protocols and sees Jewry and Freemasons as Satanic forces, both out to dominate the world. He sees nothing wrong with armies of Holy Ghost Fathers and other priests and missionaries setting off to spread their compromised message. That seems to be the trouble with imperialists, all other practitioners of imperialism drive them mad.

Eugene let out a long low whistle, which was more articulate than anything else any of us could put into words. Of course, Fahey's name wasn't new to us. To think of him influencing a generation of young clerics heading off into the mission fields was disturbing.

I hope you are relating what I am saying to your earlier policy of neutrality in this country?' he asked. 'Ignorance is surely bliss'.

'The rallies held by the Nazis – like the famous one at Nuremberg were held throughout Germany. Why were they held? Their primary purpose was to dazzle, to entrance people, to overawe them, to shake them to their foundations. When they can mount such precise, regimented and choreographed extravaganzas of public theatre, everyone is mezmerised. During one of our talks on the mass psychology of fascism we were shown, as an example of how to dominate the public mind, some old newsreels of the 1932 Eucharistic Congress in Ireland. The serried ranks of clerics processing down O'Connell Street reminded me of the theatricality of the Nazi rallies. The Romans had a name for such brainwashing control mechanisms– Bread and Circuses they called it. Fill the belly with bread: fill the mind with lies'.

One of our number Bridget asked if many of the soldiers believed in this stuff.

'I'm afraid most of them do', Johannes said. 'It's very convincing, very hard to argue with. The human mind craves answers to the big questions of life that plague us all. And certain people, political and religious demagogues and manipulators have sedulously exploited two powerful emotions, fear and anger, for as far back as we know. They provide simplistic, irrational answers to difficult questions. They articulate their arguments in such a way as to convince gullible, suggestible people, people who have been cheated of a decent education, whose minds have atrophied, that they are really quite bright for being able to follow such a complex argument, when the truth is, an average ten-year old with a bit of common sense could pick such baloney, to use one of your words, asunder. Hitler uses techniques akin to mass hypnotism, I believe. He has hammered home the same vile message, slogan by slogan, time after time after time until the people thought they were hearing it for the first time. I heard him myself whipping-up the masses, getting them worked up and you'd have to be mentally strong not to be drawn in. People get mentally drunk on such brainwashing. Can I just say while I am on the subject of discrimination of various forms, there is myth that Hitler snubbed Jesse Owens at the 1936 Olympics. Hitler didn't meet Owens, but Owens did complain bitterly about the treatment he received back home, and from Franklin D Roosevelt himself. So, we all have racial skeletons in our cupboards'.

There were nods of general agreement with this observation. There was a strong anti-semitic, anti-negro mentality in the Irish. There is nothing more smug than the holier-than-thou brigade who pile all their prejudices on to others. Some of the jokes we told each other, and the rhymes we were happy rattle-off, were too of a decidedly dubious nature. Who among us hasn't racial skeletons in their cupboards? Jesus said something about beams and motes, in our own eyes, and in others. He also had something to say about whited sepulchres.

When we had finished, and most of the group had dispersed, a few of us were in the habit of hanging back to finalise our deliberations.

Johannes said: 'Before I go, can I say a few words about the situation over at the Barracks? There is just a skeleton crew running the place now. This is true for all installations on these islands. The truth is if the people were to rise up and attack these places, I believe they could be relatively easily taken over. But please, please, don't. I'm not advocating that. Under no circumstances should anyone attempt anything so stupid.

Our surplus personnel are being directed to the Finnish and the Russian frontiers. There have been some savage things going on in places like Stalingrad, since '42/'43. The casualties are incalculable. The city is a hollowed-out, wasteland, bomb-site. But the Russians have prevailed. And still Hitler persists in his psychopathic strop, believing that he can fulfil his madman dream of Lebensraum by the subjugation of the boundless wilderness of Russia, and probably more importantly, immediately for him, control of their natural resources, oil in particular. He believes that the pounding the Russians have taken in Stalingrad has sapped both their resources and their national will. He surely knows, he must know, that every woman in Moscow, young and old, is engaged in digging huge anti-tank trenches around the city. Personally I think he has vastly underestimated the resilience of the Russians. Every available able-bodied soldier of ours who is capable of shouldering a gun and pulling a trigger is being rushed over there. But the whole project is shot through with difficulties. Our way through to Russia is being blocked by the re-conquest of lands we held earlier. This is clearly the last throw of the dice for an increasingly unhinged Hitler. It would be a mercy to us all if the lunatic were assassinated, and all of us put out of our misery. But he exercises such mesmeric control that a new conspiracy to kill him, like the one that failed, cannot get off the ground. The sooner Germany surrenders the better for the world. In the meantime the insane plan to humiliate Russia goes on.

'How can you know so much about what is going on, Johannes?' Paul asked.

'Believe it or not, pigeons have been central to the spread of information across enemy lines and not just in this War', he said. 'When it is all over, much will come to light? Fascinating stories!

But, what I wish to say to you now is that I have no intention of sacrificing myself up to realise the schemes of this demented maniac. What I and a few more of my close friends would like to know is, if we desert, first, will the people of the town accept us, and second, is there a safe place where we can hide?

'I know the very place', I said. 'In Rossadrehid'

April 2nd 1945.

I was asleep when the pebbles were thrown against the window. I looked out to see Johannes and some others standing in the garden, sheltering behind the hedge. I was downstairs in seconds.

'The main evacuation is starting', he said. 'We have managed to slip away. We were meant to be travelling on these Zundapps, which will need to be hidden. May we get out of these disgusting uniforms, please?'

They had smuggled civvies out some days before and were soon out of uniform.

'What will they do when they find you are missing?' I asked.

'Hopefully they won't discover until they arrive at Rosslare. If we are lucky, and that happens, it will be too late to do anything about us. But in the meantime is it possible to go into that hiding place you spoke of? Can we risk driving these motorcycles up to Rossadrehid?'

'We have no choice' I said. I know the back roads. We'll have to be ready to 'abandon bike' at short notice if necessary.'

'We kicked the bikes into life and headed off. We travelled by the light of the moon. Part of our route was out the Bansha road, over Longford Bridge, up the back hill, close by the tall walls of the Barracks, which fortunately were unguarded. We were soon out of the town's environs, past Brookville, and into the relative safety of the woods.

When we arrived at our destination, it was only a matter of negotiating a few narrow bohereens, opening a few gates and we were knocking on the door of our 'safe house'.

The farmer was with us in a moment. 'Good to see you, Seamus', I said. 'I have the consignment here for you'.

Seamus was an old friend whom I had often helped with the hay and the harvests. He had shown me, some years earlier, a dugout used by men on the run in the dark days of the War of Independence. They had dug into the soft Aherlow clay and excavated a sizeable souterrain in the ditch. There were butter-boxes for seats. The four Germans thought it an elegant lodging.

'You are honoured to use this facility, gentlemen', said Seamus. 'The men who used it before you were also fighting a different kind of tyranny'.

'Thank you, sir', said Johannes. 'We shall never forget this kindness and we shall repay you generously'.

'I'll be back with the tay and sangwidges', said Seamus as we made our way back to the house to conceal the Zundapps. The day was dawning as I bicycled back to town. There was a steady stream of lorries, trucks and motorcycles heading eastwards, from points west, from Clare, Limerick, Kerry, towards Waterford and Rosslare. How many of those men would be alive in a month's time was anybody's guess.

Chapter 21

... the naked Emperor ...

The Emperor of Japan addressed his people on the day of the Vernal Equinox. Such days, known as Koreisai, Holy Days, when people paid respects to past emperors and to members of imperial families, were days held in high esteem by the Japanese people. He had been advised to issue his thoughts by a letter, to be broadcast on the radio. But instead he insisted on going through with the painful task in person. He mounted the platform ponderously.

He chose as his setting the ancient Shimogamo Shrine, dedicated to gods of thunder in the old imperial capital of Japan in Kyoto, which dates back to the 7th century or earlier. It was on the Takamikura, the Chrysanthemum Throne upon which he had been enthroned as Emperor in 1926.

The trim figure of Hirohito looked burdened as he ascended the platform. He was 44 years of age, but he looked like a much older man. His son Akihito aged 12 could be seen standing to attention some paces behind his father.

'My dear people, he began. 'I stand before you a much reduced figure'. He spoke slowly, haltingly, but with gravitas in every word. 'I have been visited by representatives from America, Britain, Russia and China. They have all presented me with the same incontrovertible reality. And that is, that this war is lost.'

He seemed almost unable to get the words out. He was shaking.

'I have had time to reflect on my country's decision, on my decision, to join in with the Axis Powers, in late 1940. I would like to make it clear that the decision wasn't taken lightly. But it was ultimately my decision. And I have to tell you now that it was a wrong, a grievously wrong decision'There was a long pause, during which he stared vacantly, as if he had lost the thread of his thinking. Eventually he continued...

'Why did I take it?

There is no other way to tell this but to put it in blunt, unvarnished language. I listened to those advisors who were telling me that because of the runaway success of the Wehrmacht in the early years of the War, this was a bandwagon which Japan should, indeed must, be on. I must say I was also advised not to take that course, but I chose to go with Germany. Therefore I take full responsibility. Not one of my generals is to blame. As you know it was my oft-stated dream to expand the Japanese empire into Asia and into Russia. When I saw how Germany was bestriding the narrow world like a colossus, to quote Shakespeare, I took this as an omen that we could seize the day and bring China and Russia to heel. I madly dreamed that the Third Reich of Herr Hitler and the Japanese Empire could divide the world in half, carving up Russia in the process, thus ensuring the demise, for all time, of that unwieldy entity.

My dream, I'm sorry to say, has turned out to be a hideous nightmare. The Chinese have not forgotten our excesses in Manchuria, nor forgiven us. And why should they?

When I heard in 1941/42 that the German presence, in Ireland particularly, that country which has had such a troubled history, was being accepted by the people, I felt confident that the Third Reich could extend its sway wherever it turned its sights.

Then when it began to dawn on me in 1942 and '43 that instead of a single world war, that there were two wars going on, a Western War and an Eastern War, I realised that the Axis Master-plan to conquer the world was coming apart. We grievously underestimated our enemies.

My dear people I am addressing you openly, publicly and personally today for one main reason. And that reason is to declare the surrender of Japan to the Allied Powers. We have been given the honour of doing this in our own way, but it is surrender, nevertheless. What follows is a matter for the Allies. We can only hope to be treated humanely. I shall accept my fate. I am speaking to you to express my shame. We are a warrior, militaristic nation and words like surrender and defeat do not fall easily from our lips. For some time I have lived with the thought of ending my life violently, but have decided that to live with the shame is a greater punishment. Suicide is only honourable when done for the right reasons.

I have been told on good authority by the representatives I have met, that the war effort of Germany is being crushed in the fastnesses of Russia as I speak. It is only a matter of days before Hitler is arrested, along with what remains of his High Command.

My precious people, what sort of madness have we all lived through? Why did I ever accept the absurdity of allowing the Japanese people to be designated 'Honorary Aryans'? I rue that day. And what sort of insanity impelled the Germans to ever conceive of such a deranged notion? They have massacred millions in their death camps. I knew that was going on. I let it happen. I did not, to my shame, speak out. If Hitler had prevailed and the exterminations had proceeded apace, what long-term guarantee did we have that the so-called 'privileged category of Honorary Aryan' would have been honoured in perpetuity, when he was hell-bent on wiping out great swathes of people of the same racial type as ourselves? Whatever I am, shamed as I am, I am no anti-Semite.

We do have our ancient differences with certain neighbours - Russia, China, Korea, even America - but the idea of herding them industrially into gas chambers could never become part of our way of life. We can be ruthless, and have much to be ashamed of. But gas ovens? No.

My dear people, I bitterly regret the attack on Pearl Harbour. Again we had issues with America but what we did was beneath us. America was a sleeping giant and should have been left sleeping. The fact that American troops and ordnance are flooding into Europe as I speak, alongside Chinese, Indian, African and the remnants of the British forces, who have heroically concealed considerable consignments of military hardware in mine-shafts, in slate quarries, in caves, in underground bunkers, much of it under the Germans' very noses, in readiness for the final crushing of the head of the snake, is, I now believe, something the world will rejoice-at in times to come. The world which would have come into being following an Axis victory would, it must be admitted, have brought only savagery, misery, brutalism and repression.

We could fight on, my dear people, but it would only lead to more senseless butchery – of our own people and of our enemies. I say enemies. They are not enemies. We designated them enemies. We made them hate us because of our treatment of them. We are not free from the accusation of thinking of certain peoples as lesser beings. But if we have, that is now firmly in the past. All school texts will be revised to expunge such wrong theories. We as a nation are finished with expansionist ambitions, in Manchuria, in the Pacific, or elsewhere. We are, in the future, going to live within our own borders and going to devote ourselves to pursuance of the fruits of civilisation. We Japanese are a brilliant people and we will surprise and enrich the world with the genius of our inventiveness.

I have been warned by the representatives I've met that if we fail to surrender, an awful retribution for our crimes will be exacted. I don't need such a warning in issuing this surrender. I am issuing it because of the realisation that we allied ourselves with the most sinister forces the world has probably ever seen, and a warning was not necessary in prompting us to pull back from the cliff's edge before all is lost.

On my way here this morning, I walked along the Tadasu no Mori, the Forest Where Lies are Revealed. How could I pass through such a place and not reveal to you, my dear people, the truth, the whole truth and nothing but the truth? There is an old folk tale told about the Emperor's New Clothes, about how a foolish, conceited emperor was duped into believing that he was arrayed in the most expensive finery when he was in fact stark naked. '

He hesitated.

'I, my dear people, am that spiritually naked emperor.

I am also offering my resignation as your emperor. I am renouncing the claim that I am descended from the sun goddess Amaterasu. Such beliefs are for now and the future, children's fairy stories. The harsh winds which have howled in the recent past have taken away with them all such baseless pretensions.'

A cry arose from the multitude 'No, No, No – Ee ye, Ee ye, Ee ye'. Tears cascaded from the eyes of those incredulous people. Any single one of the revelations which they had heard would have been more than enough to traumatise them.

The Emperor stood in silence, head bowed tears streaming down his face. The wailing went on and on. Finally, when he thought the crowd was exhausted with grief, and realising the intensity of the people's loyalty, he held his hand up to quell the keening.

'My beloved people, Thank you. Perhaps my resignation is a decision for a later date. But if I do remain in office, it will be as one of you and not as a divine figure. I must be honest with you about that.

Clapping and cheering broke out. It went on for a long, long time. When it petered out stillness descended on the vast concourse.

Hirohito stood erect, like a statue, staring into space. He maintained this posture for almost an hour. There wasn't a murmur from the crowd. The wind could be heard whistling through the ornate multiple roofs of the pagodas. Birdsong punctuated the stillness. Cherry blossom drifted down.

Hirohito silently stepped backwards, bowed, and left, holding his son Akihito's hand.

Chapter 22

... the truth shall set you free...

'Captain' Jack Boyle in Juno and the Paycock neatly summed up the parlous state of things when he declared at the end of the play that 'the whole world is in a terrible state of chassis'. When Pope Pius XII came before the crowd, estimated at close to 100,000 souls in St Peter's Square on that Easter Sunday morning of 1945, it was in the expectation that he would pour the chrism of healing into hurting hearts and muddled minds.

The Encyclical was called Humilem Massae Manducare, which was quickly rendered by the wags as 'Eating Humble Pie'. By encyclical standards it was short, a mere eight pages. It briefly outlined the evolution of various elements of the Catholic Church's teaching, on how it perceived itself and how, throughout history, it had required the Faithful to think about the unique family of faith they had been either born into, or converted to.

Every Catholic boy and girl, in preparation for First Holy Communion was taught in the Creed that they were members of the world's foremost spiritual organisation. There was no other grouping on the face of the earth that one could feel so good about belonging-to, as one should feel about being a Catholic. To fall away from the Church was a grave sin, but to be excommunicated was to guarantee that one's eternal soul was lost and merited certain damnation in hell. These frightening teachings were enough to terrify most impressionable young minds, panicking them into clinging to Mother Church's apron-strings for dear life, especially eternal life, but definitely for the duration of one's earthly life.

The Pope, an austere man, read the text of his Easter message that year, 1945. It stunned the world. It was like a bolt from the blue. Can it be true people were asking each other, that we are no longer the one, holy, catholic and apostolic church? That's exactly what we are, came the answer, one, holy, catholic and apostolic, but no longer One, Holy, Catholic and Apostolic. The capitalising of the O, the H, the C and the A was what had caused all the difficulties. There was no problem with the idea of being 'one'. Why shouldn't it be 'one'? The problem arose from giving people the arrogant belief that it was THE ONE-AND-ONLY. That's what caused the friction. The Pope was now saying that the unity, the oneness of the Christian family was what we should all be striving for, that the hammer-headed zealots of the past, the schismatics on all sides, had merely been feeding their own egos, writing smarter books than one another, and playing games with the teachings of Jesus, who didn't have a theology degree, and which, if truth be told, one doesn't require a theology degree to grasp his essential teachings. These eternal truths, when boiled down are: mind your tongue, mind your own business and mind you respect others. The abandoning by the Catholic Church of the ex-cathedra teaching that it was the One-and-Only route to heaven was a great relief to other Christian faiths. Their clergy and their laity were suddenly on a par with their counterparts in the Catholic Church.

The 'Holy' bit was also easy to deal with. All religions were henceforth to be seen as equal paths to holiness, and holiness was now achievable whichever religion, church or denomination one belonged to. The Jews were no longer beyond the pale and to be subjected to vilification because their religion, like all religions was now equal to all others. All the deicide and Blood Libel lies told about the Jews were now null and void, dumped, scrapped and jettisoned. Hinduism, Islam, Buddhism were now all valid, all equal, all to be equally respected.

Up to then the Catholics, even the lowliest, most sinful ones, thought themselves as holier than the holiest of any other faith, just like some deluded white people, however low-born thought themselves a cut above anyone who wasn't white. While the others might lay claim to one, two, even three Marks, the Catholics were on top of the pile with FOUR.

The 'Catholic' bit was always a problem to me. I was 'educated' into thinking of 'Catholic' as being opposed to 'Protestant'. While we were always in the (on the?) theological right, they were forever in the (theological) wrong; simple. But then I learned that catholic with a small 'c' meant universal, global. But, I thought to myself, all the other religions were also global in their aspirations and reach, which automatically makes them catholic. So there is nothing uniquely catholic about the Catholic Church. It's catholicity has to do with its mission to convert, its objective being to 'save' the whole world, having first shepherded all humans onto the one correct path to salvation. I was further confused when I found out that sectors of the Anglican church still described themselves as Catholic with a capital 'C', after jumping ship. ('How dare they?' I heard my inner bigot still protesting.)

With regard to 'Apostolic', we really got to the crux of the matter. According to this 'Mark', the Roman church claimed to be the pure, undiluted, kosher, (wrong word), authentic faith, tracing its roots back to the twelve apostles and through them to Jesus himself. When I was required to say the Creed at mass, I wondered if poor old Jesus had any idea of what he was setting in motion? (But then I was informed that Jesus, being God, knew everything – but didn't let on. So why did he set the whole bandwagon moving? The thought wormed away in the brain). The breakaway Greek, Russian and Protestant factions were seen by Rome to have snapped the taproot which was connecting them with the true Roman teachings of Jesus, thereby forfeiting the right to the

'Apostolic' Mark. Now this Encyclical stated that they, along with the Roman church, were from henceforth, all to be seen as entitled to claim the four Marks and that Rome in its arrogance was actually the one in error, not them. This climb-down automatically removed the prejudice against clerical orders; it reinstated the freedom for clergy to marry; it paved the way for a female clergy; it instituted rights which it was hoped would cut out the anti-woman cancer that pervaded Christian writings way back to old misogynists like Tertullian, Origen, Augustine, Aquinas, Luther, and respect people's, mainly women's, freedom of conscience on rights like contraception and, the thorniest of the lot, abortion in certain, limited circumstances. The Pope exhorted the other faiths to abandon their own entrenched prejudices against women. Practices such as 'churching' women after childbirth, borrowed from the Jewish ceremony of Purification, would be abandoned, forthwith.

This encyclical was a turning point in the history of world religion. No longer need the faiths be suspicious of each other. The lurking reasons for such suspicions were now a thing of the past. If any was seen to be proselytising for reasons of numerical world domination they were deemed to be disrespecting the spirit of the new dispensation, and doing themselves a disservice. Muslims were particularly out of order on the matter of how they dealt savagely with apostates, just like the Christians had done in past centuries. (There was an apology for the Spanish Inquisition.) Now the freedom of the human individual was to be elevated to a level never before known in world jurisprudence. Matters like circumcision, male and female could now be openly debated because the whataboutery of previous ages was removed. The freedom to choose marriage partners, and to divorce unsuitable partners in state, not Sharia courts was to be universally established. The freedom to opt out of the faith which one was randomly born into was no longer to be an issue. Neither was the freedom to be an unbeliever any longer anybody's business but that of the person concerned. The Catholic Church was abandoning its ne temere decree which forced non-Catholic partners to agree that all children be brought up as Catholics. The Pope did say that the Church would continue to promote traditional principles, such as the family, as these were most likely to conduce to the well-being of the individual and to society – but as choices, not as diktats. Believers who sincerely exercised their own consciences would not, in future, be excluded from the Sacraments.

The reasons given by the Pontiff for his change of heart had to do with the descent into barbarism he had observed since Hitler came to power. He acknowledged the weight of responsibility which Christendom, particularly his own Catholic Church bore, for hacking at the roots of human rights and freedom of conscience, with its blinkered teachings, masquerading as enlightenment. He admitted how painful it was, in pointing the finger at fascism, to have to admit how culpable his own church was, particularly on the question of the Jews, in creating the ground in which fascism thrived, and reminded his audience that while one finger was pointing forward, three were always pointing back at ourselves. He declared his pride and gratitude that there were some in the Vatican itself who had defied the fascists and saved many Jews and other fleeing souls.

In presenting the Encyclical to the world, the Pope issued an invitation to the leaders of the world's great faiths and their representatives, to assemble in the Vatican in 1950, for a World Council, to begin seriously the work of reaching out to one another. 'There is little point in hermetically concentrating on reforming ourselves from within when we can at the same time be extending our reforms throughout the faiths of the world. 'We have just witnessed the consequences of what happens when rogue philosophies fester in isolation', he said, to tumultuous cheers in St Peter's Square. 'It is up to us to begin the arduous work of creating a world free from arrogance, free from the presumption of superiority, free from condescension. The Catholic Church is taking the first step in ending the conceit of so-called 'Catholic Education'. There is henceforth no such thing as Catholic education, nor Jewish, nor Muslim, nor Hindu, nor Steiner education. Nor state education. There is only education, open-agenda, open minded, inclusive, inquisitive. Schools should teach about religion but not be indoctrinating the young. Neither should governments be in charge of schooling. Independent panels of educationalists should be monitoring education in intellectually free environments, in all countries of the world. Education, like Health, should be state funded but not state administered.

There was a paragraph about literal interpretations of the Bible. He referred specifically to the dramas that surrounded the last days of Jesus. He encouraged people to see the demise of Jesus in its historical context, even referring to the role of the little-known Sejanus in Roman politics and how Herod Antipas and Pontius Pilate depended on him for their careers. He encouraged the Faithful to question whether the maelstrom of events that were alleged to have happened from the arrest of Jesus in Gethsemane to the death the following day was even chronologically possible, or whether the claim that he had been dead three days and three nights was to be taken literally. He was basically saying what Luther had said all those years before – read the Bible for yourself, don't take it as 'gospel' truth, and make your own mind up.

Tacked on at the end of the encyclical, almost as an afterthought, was an undertaking to abandon the monarchism of the papacy, and the Infallibility of the Papacy doctrine, to the great relief of many.

The Pope appealed to all Christian denominations to desist from claiming that the Bible was the 'word of God'. He lamented how this assertion had been used arrogantly in the past. He reminded the people that the notion of reciprocity pre-dated religion, by millennia, that, in fact, religion which is a man-made institution, had assimilated this truth from the study of animal and human behaviour.

'Henceforth, the Church will be the true servant of humanity, not its master'.

He then gave his Urbi et Orbi blessing to a bewildered, stunned, throng, went indoors, divested himself of his finery for the last time, and had his lunch.

April 1st 1945. The world noted the date. But the Pope was in no mood for fooling.

Chapter 23

... the murder machine dismantled ...

When the end came, it came quickly. It became obvious to the German High Command that the game was up in early April. Mass desertions followed a propaganda offensive by the Allies. Millions of leaflets that floated like benign snowflakes from the ether let serving personnel know that the situation in Russia was hopeless. The leaflets let the ordinary soldier know that he would walk free if he abandoned the fight. Yes, he could sacrifice himself for the Fatherland, but there was no Reich awaiting him on his return home, just abject, nihilistic, meaningless frustration and poverty. And yes, the Allies would bring the High Command to book and put them on trial for their ill-deeds. The leaflet informed them that the capture of Hitler was imminent.

Military discipline broke down. The common German soldier, that epitome of discipline and obedience realised he had been grievously duped, and that all he had been fighting for was now a lost cause, the scaffolding of the Reich, a crumbled shambles. Officers who tried to impose order were ignored or shot. Officers, alongside the lower ranks were deserting. The leaflet informed the soldiery that Ireland, England and the Western European nations were back in the hands of their own authorities; that elections were to follow; that American, Canadian, Indian, African troops were consolidating the Western defences; that Japan had capitulated on the East, and that Eastern Russia was unassailable.

On April 25th, on the River Elbe at Torgau, the Russians who had penetrated what remained of the Wehrmacht, joined up with Allied forces, in the final act of smashing the German war machine. For the first time since the opening salvoes of the Second World War, with Hitler's invasion of Poland, the German army was scissored in twain. The Russians, represented by Lt Sylvashko and the Americans, by 2nd Lt Bill Robertson posed for a photograph, which came to symbolise the brotherhood of the universal soldier, whose task, from time immemorial, is not to reason why, but to do or die. The people of Torgau were alarmed when the Russian troops entered the famous Hohner accordion and harmonica factory, the town's pride and joy, thinking they were going to ransack it, as is the wont of conquering forces. But the cultured Russians had other ideas. They armed themselves with musical instruments and put on an impromptu concert for the townsfolk. Instead of the lifeless death-rattle of gunfire, the town was charmed by Russian melodies, wafting through the war-torn streets, delighting the citizens. A singer provided the icing on the cake.

Meanwhile the Russians were also bearing down on Berlin. Hitler's invincible legions were rent asunder.

A great bedraggled pathetic cortege made its way homewards, like Napoleon's baffled battalions had, 133 years previously. All had seemed so good, so electrifying, only a short few months before. The German authorities had been filling their troops' heads with the fabrication that Western Europe was consolidated, that the Irish, even the English were compliantly conforming. Once Russia was contained, the story went, the Reich was secure and the job done. But all the while, there were those mysterious explosions, trains were blown up, arsenals unaccountably went sky high, installations were blasted to smithereens. All these strange mishaps happened without an enemy in sight. There was an enemy wearing a cloak of invisibility moving among them.

Hitler was tracked down to his bunker on April 20th, which happened to be his 56th birthday. He had planned to commit suicide but was disarmed and prevented from doing so by personnel in the bunker who became convinced that the world should be able to see this thwarted soul, and his other unrepentant fiends, in the dock. They overpowered him and Eva Braun, whom the monster had planned to take with him, and held them in confinement, watching him hawkishly until allied soldiers took him off their hands. He and his gang were tried at Nuremberg and sentenced to life in prison.

Giving evidence in his own defence he said that the greatest regret he had was in being unable to contain his impatience by postponing his obsession with taking on, and crushing Russia. 'Had I taken the advice from those who believed we should concentrate on securing the oil-fields of Iran, Iraq and Saudi Arabia, which were there for the taking with Britain and France humbled, our path into India would have been open, and there was no power on the planet then that could have stopped us', he said. 'But we wasted time and energy in baling out that buffoon Mussolini in North Africa. The Italian Resistance finished off the strutting windbag, attempting to escape to Spain. I should have had the braggart dispatched myself. I had had better men shot.

Do I regret the Final Solution? By no means! Even Churchill in 1920 was none too complimentary about the role of the Jews in the Russian Revolution. If you want my considered opinion, you should read Mein Kampf. In my days at Landsberg, I had time to carefully research and elucidate my theories. We Aryans are the Master Race, originating in Atlantis. The Aryan supremacy theory is found in the writings of Steiner, Blavatsky, and many others. Aryans are superior to blacks, yellows and Semites. Nothing can take that away from us. We came within a hair's breadth of world conquest. Unborn generations shall try again. Mark my words. We have no choice in the matter. Race and all that goes with it is in the very marrow of homo sapiens. It will dominate world politics into the far future. I also regret my delay in not properly subjugating the British and the Irish. I was playing for time to perfect the atomic bomb. We were months away from its perfection. Had we got there first London, Dublin and Paris would have been levelled and rebuilt in my image and likeness.' He returned to his hectoring ranting voice in delivering the latter. Those present got a taste of how mesmerising even a humbled Adolf Hitler could be. He had the menacing mien of a cornered scorpion.

An outcry followed the decision to spare their lives, particularly Hitler's life. There was such palpable fury at the grievous actions of this man that a swift dispatch into outer darkness seemed a kindness. It probably would have been for him, lost soul that he was. The same went for Hans Frank, Wilhelm Frick, Alfred Jodl, Hermann Goring, Joacim von Ribbentrop, Alfred Rosenberg, Julius Streicher, Martin Bormann. But Hitler was the one that people most focused on, to see that justice was done. Other counsels wisely prevailed and opposed the executions. A panel of international jurists from the Allied nations, after long deliberation, and after inputs from the Vatican and other religious groups, particularly from the Jewish faith, decided on sentences of life imprisonment. Some would go to Canada, some to Russia, to very remote locations. It was thought that this policy would give those convicted time to ponder their past lives, in time maybe to write books about their involvement in fascism. If the books contained more of the poison that had polluted their earlier thinking, it merely would go to prove how spiritually lost they were. Any deluded soul coming out of the Holocaust of WW2 who was still arguing that the mistake the Nazis made was in not perfecting more effective methods of mass slaughter was condemning himself out of his own mouth. If, on the other hand, he showed signs of cutting through the fog of crazed thinking that had so deluded the leaders of Nazism, it would go to show that time can bring its own new perspectives.

It was never disclosed who went where. It was rumoured that the prisoners would spend some years in one location, and then be transferred to other locations. They were all to be kept in strict solitary confinement. But one important thing the denial of the death penalty did was to prevent the martyrdom complex from taking root. It was on the record what these crazed men had done. It was there for all to see what sort of world they sought to bring into being, and any brainwashed idiot who was persevering with these fantasies, and sadly there were some, was quickly disabused. It was left up to the authorities of Germany, Japan and the other Axis powers how they would deal with the whys and wherefores of their reasoning for so misleading their peoples and for bringing such shame upon them., These matters were to be monitored by agencies from Allied nations, for 10 years initially.

Emperor Hirohito received a kindlier fate. He was tried, but the Russian, Chinese and American jurists, advised by their politicians, argued that because of mitigating historical anomalies, a sentence of what amounted to house arrest would suffice in his case. The Emperor's speech to his people at Kyoto was taken into account, when he had expressed fulsome and abject regret for the false path down which he had led his people. He was required to step aside as Emperor, a punishment which he had himself suggested. He was allowed to be Regent to his son Akihito, who was still young, but would need guidance until he understood the mazes of governance. Hirohito stated that even as a 12 year old, his son was unlikely to make the same mistakes that he had made, he who was over 30 years his son's senior.

Chapter 24

… a clash with the ash…

There were shots heard coming from the direction of the Barracks. The much-reduced garrison was evacuating – lock, stock and barrel. Johannes and his friends had made their way back to town to be there at the end but what they saw wasn't exactly what they'd expected.

The last trucks of soldiers were ready to leave. There were a few German personnel lying dead on the square adjoining the main dormitory building. About two dozen soldiers stood apart from the general throng.

What happened then surprised us all. Armed men appeared and took control.

'We are the Defence Forces of the Irish Free State, soon to be the Irish Republic', one of them said.

'But you are a cleaner', a German officer said, sneeringly.

'I'm certainly a cleaner now', the man said. 'And the sooner we clean you scum out of our town, the happier we all shall be. I am Lieutenant Aengus Furlong, and I am in charge of this operation'.

One of the men standing apart spoke. 'We are asking the townspeople of Tipperary if we can stay on here, please. We beg you. We do not want to take our places on these trucks, to go to the Russian, or any other front. We have had it with fascism. We want to be loyal citizens of this beautiful country. We have had nothing but kindness from the people of Tipperary. We have many skills to offer you'.

Lt. Furlong asked Johannes if the men were bona fide. 'Yes, some of them are – him, him, him ....' Johannes said. 'I have worked with them and they have confided in me. They are good men and can be trusted. I can vouch for every one of those I have pointed out, but not the rest. They deserve all they will receive.'

The German officer-in-charge looked at the number of armed men who now surrounded the departing troops. 'But.....' he stuttered, 'you are all employees at the Barracks. Where did you get those weapons?'

'We have had our personnel working at every level in these Barracks since you people arrived here', said Lt Furlong. 'We have been recording and monitoring every action of yours, you unwelcome trespassers on our hallowed land. Both the personnel of the Irish Army and the eyes and ears of the FCE have been trained on you like hawks. You must take the Irish people for absolute idiots, or as you would say Dummkopfe. Who are the Dummkopfe now, sending back those reports that the Irish were compliant untermench and that Tipperary was safely in German hands? Dummkopfe, Dummkopfe, Dummkopfe...You Fools, Fools, Fools. Do you think we would acquiesce under your banal dominance? You have all been living lies, all of you...for years. Well, the lies are over, and harsh truths have now to be faced. The Russians will not be as kind to you as the Irish have been'.

The German officer spoke again. 'If I had my way, what we would be bequeathing to you would be the ruined shell we found when we arrived in this pathetic backwater of a town'.

'Then why didn't you'? asked Lt Furlong.

Then Johannes spoke. 'Because of these', he said. 'I knew that that treacherous SS viper Baumann was planning something spectacular. I overheard him and his fellow conspirators, his Verschworen, talking last week before we got away from here'. Johannes held a bunch of keys aloft. 'These are the keys to the strong room where all explosives and ammunition are kept. There is enough dynamite there to do a lot more damage to this Barracks than the IRA ever dreamed of in their wildest fantasies'.

Baumann looked at him with fury in his eyes. 'You! You…..! You Verraterischer bastard. You traitorous bastard', he spluttered. 'You will be executed if ever again you set foot in the Fatherland'. 'Heil Hitler. Insel Affen, Insel Affen, Schweinehunde, Untermensch', they shrieked at the locals. With that his remaining ragbag clicked their heels and extended their right arms.

'What does Insel Affen mean? I think I know what the last two mean?' I asked Johannes. 'It means something like 'island monkeys' – it's usually reserved for the British. It loosely translates as volatile, cantankerous, cut-off. It's very insulting'. ('A bit rich coming from those who believed in mass exterminations', I thought to myself.)

'Time for you gentlemen to go', said Lt Furlong. 'First come forward each one of you to be searched.' All the men and their rucksacks were thoroughly searched. A number of guns and other munitions were found. 'We shall not say Auf Wiedersehen because it is my ardent hope that we shall not meet again. If any of you wishes to return in peace to this peace-loving island, you will be welcome here. But if you retain even a trace of the hatred that you have permitted to pollute your minds, please stay away. And please take our fraternal goodwill to your homeland. You are going to need it in the work of its reconstruction. If you need any skilled personnel, we have some to offer, for a limited period. And now Sir, I should like to make you a gift of something to remember us by. As some of you may have learned while you were here, our county, Tipperary has an illustrious hurling history and we are hoping to add to our tally of All-Ireland victories this very year.'

And Lt Furlong produced a hurley, draped in the blue and gold of Tipperary and a sliothar and gave them to Baumann.

Baumann, accepting, looked daggers at Furlong. 'Danke'. The rough manner in which he handled this exquisite piece of shapely technology told us what he would like to have done with it and it certainly had nothing to do with scoring goals in a Munster Final.

We stood in silence as the remnants of the garrison convoyed out of the main gate, under the Arbeit Macht Frei ironmongery. They headed down under the railway bridge and out onto the Bansha Road. It was a dismal tail-between-legs departure, in sharp contrast to their triumphal entry into our town.

Johannes handed Lt Furlong the keys. The young remaining Germans started to cheer and shout and hugged each other and shook hands with the Irish army personnel, with the Gardai, and with those townsfolk who by now had come to see these extraordinary events.

Johannes spoke with Lt Furlong. 'Lt Furlong', he began, ' Do I have your permission to carry out one remaining duty at these Barracks?'

'What is it?'

'It would give me deep and personal satisfaction to remove the chilling Arbeit Macht Frei ironwork over the main gates of the Barracks. This slogan is an abomination and will be quoted whenever people wish to remind us of this chapter of infamy in our history'.

'By all means', said Lt Furlong, 'but make sure in your zeal that it is removed carefully. It will be a reminder to future generations what we have just lived through'.

'I know a good blacksmith and ironmonger in town. He knows his trade'.

Army personnel moved into prearranged sentry positions in and around the Barracks. Not that anyone had any doubts about their sacrosanctity, now or in the future. They would have been as safe as the Rock of Cashel, sentry or no sentry. But nobody was taking any risks.

Johannes made his way back to the town. As he passed the railway station he saw Margaret running towards him.

Chapter 25

... Cuilin and Fachtna at the Aras ...

I was half-way through my first term at University College Dublin, in the Faculty of Architecture. Roisin was into the 4th year of her medical studies. Getting back into normal life was a challenge I relished after the dramas of the 'Emergency'.

Roisin was well-established in Dublin so I had to be patient in fitting in to her life rather than expecting her to adapt to mine, while at the same time, creating a life of my own. I knew from the first lectures that I was in the right area of study.

I received a letter in late October with the Oireachtas stamp on it. My heart always speeds up when I see the sight of an official letter in case someone has spotted me without a light on my bicycle, or not having a dog licence, or reading the wrong sort of book, or some other felonious transgression.

A Chara, it read.

Mr de Valera would like to invite both Mr Thomas Sheehan and Miss Roisin Watson to a gathering at Aras an Uachtarain, to be officiated over by an tUachtarain Mr Sean T O'Cheallaigh on Thurs Nov 15th 1945 at 3 PM.

Le meas

Eamon de Valera

Taoiseach

RSVP

I had hardly finished reading it when there was a knock on the door of my lodgings. It was Roisin.

'Did you read your letter?' she asked.

'Yes', I answered, ' What is it all about?'

'No idea', she said. 'But we'd better go, I suppose'.

'I'll reply then'.

'Now I must go or I'll be late for an autopsy', she said.

'Better you than me', I said. 'I'm happier with keystones'.

'I shall have to get permission to be away from my duties on that day', she said.

'Likewise'.

'Bye'. And she pedalled furiously away down Ontario Terrace, past Lower Mount Pleasant Avenue, heading for Portobello Bridge.

When we arrived at the Aras, who should be at the gate but the two stalwarts from the Dail! They'd presumably been promoted. Or demoted!

' Musha look who's here Cuilin? Well if tizhn't the Tipp tourists again. An' pfwhat would yee be wantin' dish time?'

'We're here to see Mr O'Kelly, An tUachterain'.

'Be the hokey farmer, Fachtna. It's the Prezhidint this time. Dey're goin' up in de world. Would yee not be waishtin' important people's time'?

'We were invited by Mr de Valera.' The two rang in and an official came out to meet us. Cuilin and Fachtna's mouths fell open.

The scene inside was breathtaking. We'd never seen anything remotely like such a gathering. Mr de Valera started proceedings by welcoming a long list of dignitaries. We began to wonder what we were doing there, but he did eventually get to us. He made a big fuss of us, to our cringe-making embarrassment. He spoke about our letter to him and about our interview nearly five years before. He went into some detail about how he had been confronted with the stark realities of the time by what we had to say.

He wound up that part by saying that there was another special guest to introduce. Everyone looked about in anticipation. Who should emerge from a side door but Winston Churchill. Rapturous applause broke out, for although Mr Churchill had been soundly defeated by Labour in the British General Election, everyone knew that the service he had rendered during the War would immortalise him.

'A Uachterain, a Thaoisig', he said in his best Irish, 'I am proud to be here today. I heard from Mr deValera about these two remarkable young people during one of our many talks in Colditz. It warmed the cockles of my heart, during those dark days, to hear of such rare gifts. He told me about their unique contribution during the recent shocking trials and tribulations, which are now happily behind us.

I am delighted to see such a large delegation of representatives from Ulster Unionism here today, and to know that the plan to re-member Ireland is proceeding apace, amicably. Who knows, Mr Taoiseach, maybe you will be calling on the Unionist bloc to join you in coalition after the next Irish election? The genius of Ulster will be a great boon to Ireland, and long overdue.

When I heard that the names of the two young people were Roisin and Thomas, I thought they were well named. And now we have more arrivals.'

At this point we were joined by more guests, and by our families, invited unbeknownst to us. And Tim Enright, Bob Noonan, Ken Hughes, and their wives and families, Johannes and Margaret. Roisin's aunt and uncle from Rathmines were there. 'I see now what you meant by if anything came of your visit to Dev', her uncle said. Much applause.

'My Irish friends tell me that one of the most cherished of all Irish Airs is Roisin Dubh – the Little Dark Rose, the Dark Rosaleen of James Clarence Mangan. And indeed our own Roisin is another Little Dark Rose.'

And with that one of his aides stepped forward with a bunch of dark inky roses and Mr Churchill and Mr de Valera together presented them to Roisin who was by now sobbing openly, as was I. And we weren't alone.

Mr Churchill continued: 'I spoke with Mr de Valera when we were in Colditz about my affection for an old ballad called The Bonny Bunch of Roses. Little did I realise we would be one day presenting a bonny bunch of roses to our own dark Rosaleen.'

There was sustained applause and cheering.

'And indeed young Thomas is also well named. For Thomas was the sceptic. Mere belief was not enough for him. Thomas took no one's word for things. Thomas had to prod and poke for himself. And our Thomas also did his own share of questioning and provoking and refusing to accept the status quo.

Thank you to both of you. And thank you to the network of women and men of the FCE – Forsa Cosanta Eireannach, that ad hoc Praetorian Guard, who informally locked arms both within Ireland, north and south, and then locked arms with the Yeomanry of England, Scotland and Wales, and Free Europe, performing acts of heroism on a epic scale which will be honoured till the crack of doom.

Congratulations to both of you. As a Thank You from London, you are hereby granted the Freedom of the City of London. The Ceremony will take place at a date to be arranged.

A hUachratain, a Thaosig, Go Raibh Mile Maith Agaibh. Go Saoradh Dia Eire.'

Thunderous applause.

Dev took over.

'Thank you Mr Churchill. And as a reciprocal honour from Ireland, which as you know has no formal honours system, the Dublin City Council is also granting Roisin and Thomas the Freedom of the City of Dublin.' (Cheering and clapping). 'I am also happy to tell you that the Irish state will meet all costs of Roisin and Thomas's education in full, including post-graduate studies, retrospective in Roisin's case.

It is my great pleasure to also announce that the Government has decided to locate the new training depot for the re-formed All-Ireland Police Service in the refurbished Barracks in Tipperary. This will be a great boost to a town which has suffered economically since the demise of the old garrison there. The sight of the Irish Tricolour proudly flying where flags of occupation once sullied the view, will be a gratifying spectacle for the people of Tipperary'.

And now I hand you over to his Excellency, An tUachtaran.'

'Dia Dhibh', began Mr O'Ceallaigh.

'The righting of ancient wrongs is a matter for much rejoicing. From this day forward, Ireland is happy to play its part as a fully functioning modern state, within the British/Irish archipelago and in time within a revived Europe.

I know that relations between our peoples in the past have been at times fraught. But the recent upheavals have served to underline the strength of trust and affection that underpins our bonds. I also know that we must take our share of responsibility for how affairs were managed in the past, for things that were done and perhaps shouldn't have been done. Perhaps we in 1916 acted in haste, trying to achieve severance at a time when other crises should have been priorities for us. What we have been taught by Hitler is that the interests of Britain are also our interests, and vice versa. This will not change. We have a deeper bond between each other than to any other external power. We shall not let anything come between us in the future. Empty rhetoric is merely hot air and we have, unfortunately, had a plethora of it from romantics in Ireland. We went to war with Britain on a blinkered agenda in 1916, and managed to divide our country as a consequence. This rift is now in the process of being healed. Amen to that. The unity of The Bonny Bunch of Roses shall ne'er be broke.

We have been promised a generous Aid Plan to revive our country economically, and to put behind us, for good, the grim prospect of the emigrant ship which is what we have been offering to far too many of our young people. And we trust that Roisin and Thomas will play their part in being foremost in making this reconstruction of our country a reality.

Go raibh mait agaibh.'

The event went on into the early evening. The press was there and the subsequent publicity took some time to live down. As we left the Aras, Cuilin and Fachtna saluted us and shook us warmly by the hand. This meant a lot to us.

Roisin and I went to Tipp for the autumn break. I was keen to visit Seamus Brogan in Rossadrehid. Roisin and I headed off on our bicycles and were soon past Scallagheen and Brookville, and heading up through Ballyglass. By the time we had come over the brow of Slievenamuc, we stopped at Ballynacourty Wood, where I had spent many a summer day picking whorts, a lucrative pastime for school children with time on their hands, of which we were millionaires. We stopped to take in the grandeur of Aherlow, which never fails to stir the soul.

As Roisin and I gazed in awed silence down into the Glen, I made a genuflection. In fact I went fully down on one knee, while simultaneously and clumsily fishing a small box out of my trousers pocket. I opened it, took out its contents and said, at least I tried to say, but by them I was overcome with heaving sobs of emotion. Roisin could see what I had in my hand and it started her off too.

When I had regained a modicum of control, I began again. 'Roisin', I said, 'will you marry me? I love you so, so much'.

Roisin's dark eyes brimmed and twinkled with tears. 'Yes, Yes. Yes, Thomas', she said, 'I will. I will. I will. I love you', smiles breaking through the sobs of elation. 'I just...... '.

I knew what she was going to say – about her studies, about my studies, about how she was going to India to work at a leper colony for a year, run by the Good Shepherd Sisters, and a Ugandan hospital for a year.

I gently put my finger to her lips. I even had a better idea. I kissed her. That silenced her.

'Say nothing for now, please. We have had too many hurdles placed in front of us up to now. Let's fully enjoy this moment'.

We had a cup of tea and a slice of cake with Seamus and his wife and family. They were so happy to be first to hear our news. Seamus said that he could always call on Johannes and his friends if a heavy job needed doing in a hurry. They never failed him. He praised them to the heavens and said what a boon they were to Tipperary.

On our cycle back to town, it felt as if we were airborne.

Because we were.

Chapter 26

… underground streams surface…

If what Emperor Hirohito, and after him Pope Pius had to say took the world by storm, what was to come out of Russia, shook it to its foundations.

When the Soviet Union emerged out of the 1917 Revolution, the Left internationally was buoyed-up with the belief that out of the trauma of World War 1 had arisen a development that was the beacon mankind had been searching for. Here in embryo was the New World Order, the Great Leap Forward that put mankind on a new path – one of peace, of equality, of fraternity, of liberty. Enlightened phrases, like 'To each according to his needs, From each according to his ability' struck a deep chord in the hearts of the masses and were to be heard coming from the lips of high-minded campaigners like James Connolly, Keir Hardie, Jim Larkin, and trade union leaders the world over. It encapsulated the essence of the great faiths. The down-trodden of the earth felt their hour had come, that the meek would indeed inherit the earth – the ruling elites were going to be cast down from their seats, the humble exalted and the commanding heights of all the economies of the world, land, labour and capital were finally to be firmly in the hands of the proletariat. There would be no more dreaming of pie in the sky, now that mankind would be communally engaged in creating Paradise on earth! That great visionary Karl Marx would be vindicated. As Wordsworth had said of being alive at the time of the French Revolution, 'Bliss was it in that dawn to be alive, But to be young was very heaven'. Bliss! Heaven on Earth! That's what every idealist dreamer, north, south, east and west felt about the shifting of the political tectonic plates of the world. The removal from the world of people like the privileged Royal Family of Russia, the Romanovs, symbolised these changes, the elimination of the unfairnesses of the past. Or so Pravda said.

To set the wheels of the Revolution in motion, its architect, Lenin had to journey from Switzerland to Petrograd, via Finland, a journey which it was alleged was facilitated by Germany which at that critical time had a vested interest in destabilising Russia.

After that cage-rattler Trotsky had been ejected, like a cuckoo from the nest, following Lenin's death in 1924, Stalin set to work consolidating the gains of the Revolution. He set up a totalitarian police state. His methods weren't pretty, but he convinced the masses that to secure the Revolution, counter-revolutionary elements, fifth-columnists, enemies-within, had to be silenced. It was futile, even dangerous, to ask questions about the methods which had been used to silence them. But silent they became.

Throughout the 20s and 30s, Russia became Purgatory on Earth. Purges, show-trials, accusations, kangaroo-courts, conspiracies, ad hoc juries – became the order of the day. News travelled slowly. But news travelled. Nobody knows how many kulaks were exterminated, how many dissidents were eliminated, how many refusniks were 'disappeared', how many over-worked non-conformists starved in the gulags. And we can but guess at the numbers who died in the famine of '32/'33 while forced collectivisation was being rammed through.

Some erstwhile enthusiasts for the Revolution, among them Malcolm Muggeridge, a (then) left-wing English journalist, George Orwell, Arthur Koestler, and many, many more began to slowly see through the fog of propaganda, and have serious doubts about what was really going on, and to have serious doubts about the blandishments of Marxism in general. George Bernard Shaw visited Russia in 1931 and was completely duped by the stage-managed itinerary and VIP treatment he received. He described Stalin as 'a Georgian gentleman'. In a co-signed letter to the Manchester Guardian in 1933 he said: "No lie is too fantastic, no slander is too stale... for employment by the more reckless elements of the British press." The gullible Shaw had much influence, some would say too much. He was later to wax lyrical about Hitler and Mussolini. He seemed to have developed a partiality to 'strong men' in the autumn of his life.

The show-trial of Nikolai Bukharin following the Great Purge of the '30s was the last straw for those surviving Russians who had woken up to the evils of Stalinism. Had not Hitler's war games prolonged Stalin's life by some years, the moderates would have asserted themselves earlier.

By the end of the war, a head of steam, embracing every level of Russian society, had built up about the direction in which the country was headed. Those whom Stalin had labelled counter-revolutionaries mounted a campaign to hold two referendums. The spreading of these ideas was an underground, samizdat activity, to begin with, but as critical mass built up, the media became more and more emboldened. It was insisted that the ballot be strictly private, and in sealed booths, something the Russian people had been deprived of, party 'activists' having hung around polling stations to make sure that people voted for 'The Party'.

The first Referendum asked the simple question: 'Do you agree with the way in which Russia is being presently governed?'

For the second referendum to be triggered there had to be an over two-thirds Yes or No vote. There was a resounding 85% No vote returned.

This outcome triggered the second Referendum, which turned out to be an historic experiment in democracy, to be later copied by countries all over the globe. It was a multi-option referendum and contained the following questions:

1 Is communism working for Russia?

2 Should private property be a human right?

3 Should freedom of religion and freedom of conscience be human rights?

4 Are Five Year Plans the best method of running an economy?

5 Would you encourage the spread of Russian communism to every country in the world?

6 Do you personally know of anyone who has lost their life, property, or rights in Russia in recent decades?

7 Do you believe in totalitarian government?

8 Did you agree with the execution of the Romanov family?

9 Should Russia adopt liberal capitalism?

10 Do you agree that Russia should be a liberal democracy with functioning political parties?

11 Do you agree with freedom of speech?

12 Would you be in favour of introducing proportional representation?

13 Do you agree with the secret ballot?

14 Do you agree with forced collectivisation?

15 Do you believe that those deprived of property by the Russian state should have it restored to them?

16 Does Communism stifle private enterprise?

The ballot paper was designed so that the voter could write 10 if they agreed strongly, down to 0 if they disagreed strongly with the proposition, with intermediate numbers for those in doubt.

The results were overwhelming. Most questions got an 80/20 in favour decision – some 90/10. Russia was on a new and democratic road. Stalin was utterly discredited. He and his henchmen had done their utmost during the campaign to confuse, to confound, to twist, to distract, to fake, to bully, using all the old propaganda tactics that had kept him in his autocratic position in the past. Language had been the main casualty of their bending of the truth. They called their paper Pravda, the Truth, which was the sickest joke the embattled people had ever heard.

Stalin, the Man of Steel, was no more. He was tried for crimes against the Russian people. There were so many people offering to come forward to give evidence against this despot that the trial could have gone on a long time. As with Hitler, there were cries for vengeance. But Joseph Vissarionovich Stalin, born Ioseb Besarionis dze Dzhugashvili, one-time would-be priest, turned atheist, turned megalomaniac, was allowed to live out his life in a draughty dacha in Siberia, named Ekaterinburg, lest he be allowed to forget, where he pottered in obscurity and pondered his grizzly life. He never renounced his convictions. He was allowed generous rations of tobacco and vodka. He did not live long.

Russia, ever grateful for the support of Allied friends, formed bonds of fraternity with the West, and the East. Exchanges of students, travellers, ideas, goodwill, firmly placed the post-war world on the path of peace. The reforms enjoyed by the Russian people took root in China, to the great benefit of the world's population, yielding stability and order.

Chapter 27

... the longing for a Homeland...

The stories that were filtering through from the concentration camps caused me to look more searchingly into the whole Jewish experience in Europe. I developed a strong empathy with this maligned people. One comment by Chaim Weizmann to the Peel Commission, set up in 1936, which turned out to be ominously prophetic, was that there were in Europe 6,000,000 Jews ... "for whom the world is divided into places where they cannot live and places where they cannot enter." ... Places where they cannot live and places where they cannot enter.....I had heard many odious references to 'The Wandering Jew', usually from people of ill-intent, and Weizmann's sad observation had a dismal echo to it.

Had the war not intervened, the outbreak of conflict between Arab and Jew in the late 1930s was a wake-up call to the world that all was not well in Palestine. The collapse of any empire leaves a menacing vacuum in its wake and the implosion of the Ottoman Empire created a climate of anomie in Palestine.

The trickle of Jewish immigrants into this ancient land in the 20th century alarmed Arabs. Hostilities broke out seriously in 1936 and enquiries were set up by the British into the causes. Common sense would have told them that the reason why unrest grows has most likely to do with people feeling threatened, or dispossessed, or impoverished, shorn of rights, and the old faithful, xenophobia, is never far away. The sulphurous animus between Arab and Jew snaked back into Old Testament times; The Woodhead Commission came up with the standard treatment for such tensions, namely: Partition. When in doubt, draw lines on maps. This brilliant ruse had been employed by the parties at the Berlin Conference in 1884 as a solution to the 'Africa problem'. The resources-hungry expansionists of Europe had taken out their straight-edges and carved straight lines through the heartlands of the African continent, contemptuous of the consequences. It was reminiscent of the Treaty of Todresillas of 1494, when the then Pope, Alexander VI, of unhappy memory, in a feat of breath-taking arrogance divided the newly discovered world between Portugal and Spain, to the exclusion of those nations who would soon be classifying themselves as Protestant, and who would have something to say about such blinkered haughtiness. The Sykes-Picot Agreement of 1916 was another exercise in drawing lines on maps, this one outlining British and French spheres of influence following an Ottoman Empire defeat in the First World War.

And the skew-whiff, bockety line on the Irish map was another acknowledged masterpiece of its kind.

It was ironic that the promise contained in the Balfour Declaration of 1917, calling for the establishment of a homeland for Jews, was a Lebensraum of sorts. The roots of Jewish traditions in these regions went back as far as any other groups who populated them, but that didn't mean that friendly co-existence had been enjoyed. Even a cursory glance at the Old Testament, one serial concatenation of siege and besiege, told you that. Who was David, and who Goliath? That was the conundrum.

Jews had strayed far and wide throughout the planet, and not always receiving an open-arms welcome. The growth of the ideology of Zionism, which expressed the Jews' longing for a homeland, expounded by Theodor Hertzl who was a leader of the movement in the late 19th century, gave momentum to pressure on governments to create a state where Jews could feel secure.

The events in Europe from '39 to '45 dramatically changed attitudes to the plight of the Jews. The plan to create a Jewish homeland was rejected by the Arabs, one of whose leaders was Amin al-Husseini. Al-Husseini had backed Hitler and Mussolini during the War, as did much of the Arab world. Hitler had the same contempt for the Arabs as he had for Jews, as Islam would have found to its cost had Germany prevailed.

In 1945 things looked very different. A United Nations Conference on the Palestine dilemma was convened. It was decided that a One State solution to the Israel/Palestine conundrum was the only way forward, one that guaranteed the forestalling of future aggravations. Various permutations and combinations of non-contiguous parcels of land calling themselves Arab Palestine were proposed, but on consideration, were rejected as unworkable. In order to create a permanent, secure settlement to this age-old problem, the major voices of the United Nations decreed that the sharing of the area, bordering on Lebanon, Syria, Transjordan, Egypt, and with the full backing of those nations, was essential for enduring stability. Al Husseini had been assured by Hitler of ongoing support once victory had been achieved, support which, needless to say, did not envisage fair play for Jews. His serious miscalculation about the course and outcome of the War undermined his heft, and that of others who wished for a much different post-war world, in the consultations which ensued, about the founding of the new state.

The United Nations replaced the defunct League of Nations in Oct 1945. This battered old world of ours was crying out for a world authority with credible powers.

The Conference on Israel/Palestine produced the following Concordat:

- The new state, called Greater Israel, would be secular.

- The strengths of the new state would be:

- It would be a democracy – a beacon in a region not noted for its democratic instincts

- It would have a secular constitution – answering zealots on both sides, and blunting their extremist impulses.

- It would share the whole Israeli/Palestinian land mass.

- The problem of Jerusalem as either a Jewish or Arab capital would be solved, because of shared governance.

- There would be a central, common authority.

- There would be agreement, with external, international monitoring, on the vexed matter of planning and land-use.

- There would be no "peace" walls

- There would be no need for terrorism, because of universal consensus with the nature of the state, and support from neighbours.

- There would be no ungovernable pockets of non-contiguous land.

- There would be the disempowerment of extremist fundamentalist religious zealots, on all sides, of whom there were many.

- There would be a silencing of the doom-sayers who were convinced that Jew and Arab must be locked in a never-endingly bitter feud.

- No need for humiliating, aggravating checkpoints.

- There would be free movement of labour, talent and goods, but strict controls on inward immigration.

- There would be free, universal, integrated education.

The new country would be a beacon to the wider Middle East region providing much needed and craved-for stability.

There were the predictable pockets of cynics who gave the new state no chance of success. There were those who set about destabilising it, but the combined power of the Greater Israeli armed forces would soon put a stop to their gallop.

The pooling of Jewish and Arab genius soon set about constructing a state that would accommodate more citizens that anyone had earlier envisaged and the population began to expand steadily. Kibbutzim were the talk of the world and were a model for other regions striving to swim free from the undertow of a scarred history.

Arab leaders apologised for their ill-intentioned support for Fascism.

Roisin and I made plans to spend a holiday working on a kibbutz south of Beersheva, in the Northern Negev Desert.

Chapter 28

... O My Dark Rosaleen ...

We went to England on our honeymoon. We drove down through Wales, as Bob and I had done on our speculative trip all those years ago, but which now seemed like yesterday.

We spent a couple of nights in Shrewsbury, soaking up the atmosphere of that charmed place. I showed her where Bob and I had stopped, and about the Antzies' intrusion. Shrewsbury Flower Show was on while we were there, which the locals told us was the oldest flower show in the world. Roisin had never seen anything quite so breathtakingly beautiful. I told one of the rose growers what Roisin's name meant in English. He presented her with an inky-black rose, having announced over the public address system that we were there from Ireland on our honeymoon. The Show stopped and Roisin got a loud cheer. There were countless acknowledgements of Ireland's recent role in bringing Hitler to heel. We of course said nothing of our small part, but it made us very proud to be treated with such spontaneous and genuine goodwill by those warm-hearted Salopians. It was a sign of things to come, of better relations between our peoples and so, so welcome.

We stopped in Wroxeter. There was nobody there. A balmy embracing hush enveloped us. I had taken the trouble to bring along a copy of Housman's poem about Uriconium. I read it to Roisin. I pointed out the Wrekin in the distance, the hill referred to in the poem.

Then, 'twas before my time, the Roman
At yonder heaving hill would stare:
The blood that warms an English yeoman,
The thoughts that hurt him, they were there.

There, like the wind through woods in riot,
Through him the gale of life blew high;
The tree of man was never quiet:
Then 'twas the Roman, now 'tis I.

The gale, it plies the saplings double,
It blows so hard, 'twill soon be gone:
To-day the Roman and his trouble
Are ashes under Uricon.

I couldn't wait for us to arrive at Ironbridge. As we stood on that exquisite piece of rugged, interlocking, industrial filigree we watched the solemn Severn as it made its way from the Welsh mountains to its Estuary in the Celtic Sea.

We learned about Abraham Darby and 'Iron Mad' Wilkinson, he of razor-blade fame. I quoted from an old ballad I had come across, about the craze back then for cast-iron:

Since cast-iron is now all the rage
And scarce anything's now made without it
As I live in this cast-iron age
I mean to say something about it
We have cast-iron coffins and carts
Cast-iron bridges and boats
Corn-factors with cast-iron hearts
That I'd hang up in cast-iron coats....

Roisin loved the bridge, as I knew she would. As we stood over its central arch, I proposed to her again and she accepted me again. More tears. Bridges, their symbolism and significance had come to mean a lot to us after what we had been through in recent years. We celebrated in the Tontine Hotel.

In spite of all the chaos, Roisin had graduated first in her year at Medical School and the experience she had gained in India and Africa would stand her in good stead in her future medical career.

We arrived in Birmingham at nightfall. There was much evidence of the bombings that has wreaked such havoc in the city, the third most bombed city in Britain, after London and Liverpool. We had been invited to stay with Ken and his family in Northfield. The welcome we got was deeply touching. Ken's wife, Dorothy told us about how he had spoken about the visit of Bob and I and how moved he and his fellow Yeomen had been to know that Ireland was with them.

On the following morning Ken said he'd like us to meet some friends for a get-together in Birmingham at about 11 o'clock. We took the bus into the city centre and he ushered us into what looked like civic buildings. As we entered, a brass and reed bank struck up 'It's a Long Way to Tipperary'. The place was full to capacity. Roisin and I were led on to the stage as the crowd joined in the chorus...'It's a Long Long Way to Tipperary, for my Heart lies there'.

The Lord Mayor of Birmingham was standing at the table and welcomed us. He spoke warmly of the ties that linked Ireland with that part of England since the dawn of the Industrial Revolution, about how there had been a steady influx of Irish people over the centuries, how proud the Brummies were of that link. He asked, out of interest, how many people present had some Irish in them and Roisin and I could hardly believe the number of hands that went up. The words '...their unity will ne'er be broke', again crossed my mind.

Ken spoke of Bob's and my visit all those years ago, how he and the Yeomen were reassured to know that Ireland had risen to the challenge of meeting the curse of fascism head on. The Mayor proceeded in granting the Freedom of Birmingham to Roisin and me. We were elated by this singular honour, and accepted it on behalf of the people of Tipperary and Ireland. Roisin spoke about some doctors from the West Midlands she had met in India and Africa and about continuing links in the future. I was so proud of her. I could see there and then the considerable person she had become and the great contribution not only to medicine but to women's education she was going to make.

I asked Ken if I could visit the warehouse in Digbeth, just for old times' sake. Roisin was very keen to see it as well. There was nothing very special about it, it had no particular architectural or cultural significance, but to us it was of the utmost private importance.

One of the last places Roisin wanted to see was Worcester Cathedral, which I also wished to see as I hadn't got that far on my earlier trip. It didn't disappoint. A guide took us round and pointed out features that a cursory glance might have missed, particularly its Norman to Perpendicular Gothic architectural styles, which were of increasing interest to me. He told us that the city, a Royalist stronghold during the English Civil War was proud of its reputation as 'Fidelis Civitas', The Faithful City, a motto which was emblazoned on its Coat of Arms. Roisin and I got an insight into how the memories of the English Civil War were still present in the minds of the people, as the guide was telling us how Cromwell's troops had ridden their horses into the Cathedral and vandalised it. He told us this with a degree of impacted passion in his voice. He spoke of the smashing of stained glass windows, and about how horses had been stabled in the Cathedral. I could see that he was personally affronted by this sacrilege. 'Sometimes at night, when I am here on my own, although the place has been fumigated countless times since those dark, ominous days, I believe I can still get a faint whiff of horse manure coming at me', he said, without a flicker of irony in his voice. Cromwell may be a hero to some, but he wasn't to this man. 'Ironically', I suggested to him, 'Cromwell may well have saved the monarchy for posterity. When revolutionary times came to other countries, and heads rolled into baskets, the English had already been there, the antibodies to extremism were in the system, and they weren't going back'. He reluctantly had to agree. History is a convoluted teacher. I hadn't learned much from McMehony, but I'd learned that.

We spent our last afternoon walking on the Malvern Hills. We made it to the top of The Beacon, so named because it was from this and many more summits that fires radiated through the countryside in 1588, warning of the Armada. Lord Macauley in his poem Armada, commemorates that fraught time.

And on, and on, without a pause, untired they bounded still
All night from tower to tower they sprang; they sprang from hill to hill
Till the proud Peak unfurled the flag o'er Darwin's rocky dales
Till like volcanoes flared to heaven the stormy hills of Wales,
Till twelve fair counties saw the blaze on Malvern's lonely height,
Till streamed in crimson on the wind the Wrekin's crest of light.

Much as we appreciated that rolling Beacon, the Galtees beckoned.

Roisin and I were ready to return to Ireland, to take up our posts, she building bodies, me building buildings.

Epilogue

...the Bonny Bunch of Roses,
Their unity shall ne'er be broke...

It was as if a great weight had been lifted off us all. And by 'us all', I mean, initially, the citizens of the British/Irish archipelago. The prejudices of the past, wrapped-up in those lazy stereotypes, which manifested as jokes and 'slagging', hadn't completely disappeared, but the animus that had lurked in the undergrowth of people's psyches had just run out of steam. Not that the Welsh, the Scots and the Irish had totally ceased to see the English as annoyingly and patronisingly superior, but now with the Empire gone, and England having had a bellyful of what it was like to have tasted the bitter fruits of being conquered, there was a level playing field for all.

The Irish, of whatever ilk, were ecstatic with the gift that kept on giving, which was the experience of liberation from the shadow of partition and all the ethnic- and identity-ills that had flown from that gargantuan mistake. Ulster Unionists were freed from the bondage of being a permanently besieged enclave, in a territory they insisted on calling a 'country', which they knew, and everyone else knew, wasn't a country, of being a minority on the island who behaved like a majority in their gerrymandered non-country, which wasn't even a complete province. The place had had all the hallmarks of an open political asylum, in which the inmates, untreated, slowly became madder and madder, rattier and rattier. They were now enjoying not having to pretend to be more English than the English, because both knew that that was a fiction to start with, a fiction which was exploded as soon as one of them turned up in

England, where all those emanating from the island of Ireland were correctly designated Irish. They were now free to talk openly and not defensively about why their forbears, buoyed-up by false promises, had migrated to Ulster when they did. The Protestant working class found it had far more in common with their Catholic counterparts and could engage in meaningful politics free from the sectarian backdrop so dear to 'big house' Orangeism. Generations of Ulster Protestants had to play along with the befuddling game of identifying with a leadership that cared little about them, if truth be told, but deemed necessary because of the imperative of keeping their distance from the Taigs. Such artificial divisions resulted in them living in a suffocating political cul-de-sac. They swallowed lies that they were better off than the Catholics, that their education was better, when that small voice in them told them that none of this was true. The same liberation applied to the northern nationalists, who in their turn had tried to be more Irish than the southern Irish. It freed those others on the island who had names that looked or sounded anything but 'indigenous', whatever that meant, from the suspicion that they weren't 'one of us'. True, England had given Ulster's leaders its word in 1922, but what happened in 1939 trumped all previous promises, and the Unionists accepted it. And because there was no sense of triumphalism in the south's attitude to them, the old mentalities just faded away – language like 'Black North', 'Priest-ridden South' – went out the window. The majority population on the island, were freed from that debilitating, sub-vocalised, internalised discourse it had carried on with itself for generations, an exchange which was betimes, murderous, delinquent, immature, sectarian, self-righteous, adolescent, - a dialogue which expressed itself audibly as equivocal, ambivalent, blinkered, complicit, particularly when it came to the use of violence in the pursuit of political ends... the psychic conflict, the centuries-old feud... it all just faded away. It was finally permissible to say something positive, affirmative, even affectionate, about the English/British without bringing your Irishness into question. The old game of 'taking sides' had lost its meaning.

I haven't dwelt in any detail on the many and not infrequent tongue-lashings I got from certain quarters because of the stand I took, particularly on the neutrality issue. In an island like Ireland, which produced two hermetically-sealed sectarian societies, each convinced that the other side to be the anti-Christ, it is so easy to opt for the lazy hammock of being ventriloquised, to spout the shop-soiled banalities of the puppet-masters. Joyce spotted this very early in his life and refused to be anybody's mouthpiece. Nobody's dummy he. Thank you, Shem. Not for him the cosy mantras of the echo-chamber. He was one for changing his notes from tree to tree.

'Up the Workers!, Up the Shinners!, Up the Republic!, Up Dev!, Up Duffy!, Up King Billy!, Up Carson!, Up the Pope!, ...', such inanities ceased any longer to have traction. The suffocating sheaths had been penetrated. Old Ireland was free. 'Up Down' did survive the bonfire of the shibboleths. But Down was not up there anymore. Down was now down here. We were made up when this happened. Visitors no longer needed to be told that Donegal, the most northerly county in the country was in the South but not in the North. Other venom-laden stumbling blocks like the Free State, the Six Counties, the Twenty Six Counties, the Orange State, Northern Ireland, Southern Ireland, Saorstat Eireann, (which Lloyd George had tried to catch de Valera out on, remarking that as the Irish had no word in Irish for republic, that such a concept was alien to the Irish. Dev was not amused by such trivialities. Poblacht was the word. All these contentious labels withered on the vine. Ireland (Republic of) and Eire were fine.

Notions such as north, south, east and west began to mean just that, geographical designations, not political enclaves. People in the south of County Down, who had become used to the 'South-East' meaning the area (in Northern Ireland) around the Mournes, had now to re-adjust to the South-East as meaning the real South-East, Wexford, Waterford, Kilkenny region. Travelling around the island began to be more seamless, the no-go-areas mentality being happily jettisoned. Both Ireland and Britain introduced Welfare States, of equal comprehensiveness.

Northern nationalists, who had marinated in their grievances for over 300 years had some hasty adjustments to make. No longer did their knee-jerk anti-Protestant/Unionist/British anchorages have any meaning. No longer could they huddle in their ghettoes and bemoan their plight. No longer would many of their 'rebel' songs, like When St Peter's Day was a-Dawning find any place in musical get-togethers. That song contained the lines:

Let's banish the crew that our land did pollute

And corrupted our true ordinations

And may their women all miscarry

All those who carry the rank seed of Harry...

We'll send them a-sailin' both putrid and carrion

To some other island that's fruitless and barren...

....That and all the other toxic accretions of sectarian bilge were consigned to the dustbin of history. The sulphurous rages they had sedulously cultivated no longer served any useful purpose. Schools were integrated, the bishops having been forced into a climbdown by the Vatican. Schoolbooks were re-written to expunge them, insofar as that is possible, of their hidden agendas. Those who persisted in their bigotries were isolated and seen as the neanderthals they truly were.

Now both tribes had to get out there and make a success of their place of birth, instead of parading their victimhood. The mentality of beleaguerment, so precious to the Boyne-obsessed backwoodsmen of Unionism crumbled like a sand-castle in a flowing tide.

There were sweet songs being sung. Songs of true freedom...

And Dev did invite the Unionists to join him in Coalition. And they did. And it lasted.

And Ireland did join the Commonwealth and was welcomed back with open arms.

The world breathed easier. It was as if it had, collectively, passed across a threshold, gone through a portal to a better place. Things do get better if we choose to learn from the sins of the fathers.

And from our own.

'Twas early early all in the spring
The birds did whistle, aye, and sweet did sing
Changing their notes from tree to tree
And the song they sang was Old Ireland free.

Printed in Great Britain
by Amazon